Praise for Robert G.

"Robert McBrearty's stories occupy a fascinating world where the daft becomes heartfelt, the dangerous becomes ordinary, and the ordinary becomes downright odd- and where the act of writing is appropriately worthy of awe. A world, in other words, seen through a pane of absurdist old glass."
—DAVID WROBLEWSKI, AUTHOR OF *THE STORY OF EDGAR SAWTELLE*

"*THE WESTERN LONESOME SOCIETY* is a thing of beauty, a house with many rooms, all built of humor and pathos. I don't know what to call it, comic novel or surreal novella, or a genre all its own, a literary tall tale. McBrearty's work shows an extraordinary imagination and a deeply felt love for the written word."
—BARRY KITTERMAN, NEA FELLOWSHIP WINNER, AUTHOR OF *THE BAKER'S BOY* AND *FROM THE SAN JOAQUIN*

"McBrearty's writing is simultaneously poignant and hilarious. Themes of belonging, nostalgia, and the nature of home intertwine in this deep short novella."
—FOREWORD REVIEWS

"His writing is always lovely and down-to-earth and his exuberant sense of humor blends beautifully with the very serious human realities underlying his tales....Robert's stories deliver what I think all great stories do: they illuminate what's universal in our shared human experience."
—ANTHONY POWELL, ARTISTIC DIRECTOR, STORIES ON STAGE

PRAISE FOR EARLIER WORKS

"If you tossed some Richard Brautigan, a little Charles Bukowski, maybe a dash of Walker Percy into a blender, you might get a cocktail like this." —*VANCOUVER PROVINCE*

"McBrearty has a flair for the comic." —*CHICAGO TRIBUNE*

"He writes with great heart and can play all the notes on the scale of humor." —**JENNY SHANK,** *NEW WEST*

"McBrearty writes with deep compassion for his characters, and while his stories are often wryly amusing, they leave a pleasantly melancholy aftertaste." —**CLAY EVANS,** *BOULDER DAILY CAMERA*

"The quirky, self-dramatizing characters make good progress toward redemption, or at least manage to laugh in the face of their anxieties." —*PUBLISHER'S WEEKLY*

"It's this superb mix of the dark and comic, interwoven seamlessly into the fabric of his fiction, that establishes McBrearty as a master stylist in his work as a whole." —*PRAIRIE SCHOONER*

The Western Lonesome Society

The Western Lonesome Society

A Novel by
Robert Garner McBrearty

CONUN
DRUM
PRESS

A Division of Samizdat Publishing Group

CONUNDRUM PRESS
A Division of Samizdat Publishing Group, LLC.
PO Box 1353
Golden, Colorado 80402

ISBN: 978-1-942280-12-5

Library of Congress Control Number: 2014958358

Conundrum Press books may be purchased with bulk discounts for educational, business, or sales promotional use. For information please email: INFO@CONUNDRUM-PRESS.COM

Conundrum Press online: CONUNDRUM-PRESS.COM

Cover Painting and Design: Shannon Faber (shannonfaber.com)
Author photo: Mary Ellen Metke

A portion of this book appeared in the short story "Let the Birds Drink in Peace" in the author's collection *Let the Birds Drink in Peace.*

To my beloved Mary Ellen, my treasured sons, my siblings, my father, and in memory of my mother.

I am grateful to all my friends and family for their kind encouragement over many years, but I especially wish to acknowledge my friends Tim Hillmer, David Wroblewski, and Kimberly McClintock for their generous readings of earlier versions of this book and for their good suggestions. As well, I thank my friend Tom Lamarr Jones for his encouragement over many discussions of this book and writing in general. I am also grateful for the editorial assistance of Debbie Vance and Sonya Unrein, and I thank my publisher, Caleb Seeling, for his unrelenting devotion and enthusiasm in bringing this book forth.

The Current Situation

On a warm afternoon in summer, many years after his kidnapping, in the makeshift room above his garage, in a modest, ramshackle suburban neighborhood in a small city somewhere in the West, Jim stands at the window, training a pair of binoculars on the neighborhood streets. He's watching for signs of trouble, of any threats to his own family. For now, all looks quiet on the Western front. Across the street, a woman walking a white poodle, down the block a guy on a bike, but no apparent threat in sight. He reviews the neighbors in his mind. Probably no kidnappers among them, but the neighbors make him insecure in other ways. The Wilsons across the street have great adventures. Their boy, Addell, at four, was the youngest ever to climb Pike's Peak. The Johnsons, to the south, are great humanitarians; broad-faced and beaming toothily, they are frequently pictured in the paper for their winter coat drives.

The Smiths, to the north, are simply beloved by everyone. They have seven children and each year a different one is high school valedictorian. They have a swimming pool filled all summer with family and friends and neighbors, all bouncing cheerily around.

All three families send Christmas newsletters. So many awards! So many scholarships! So many trips! So much happiness and success! How can Jim's family compete?

The Rathmans do not send Christmas newsletters. There are older children who have moved back home, husky young men who go in and out the front door carrying automotive parts. They have numerous cars and trucks parked in their driveway, in front of their house and up and down the street. They are forever working on their cars and trucks and washing them. Whenever he pulls his scraggly Toyota into his driveway, which has cracked and settled, weeds spurting through the seams, Jim waves to them if they are in their driveway working on their cars and they wave grudgingly back with wrench-filled hands.

Worrying about so many things at once is tiresome, and Jim moves from the window and lies down on an old green couch. Through motes of dust, as if materializing in a sudden glare of sunlight through the window, into the scene intrudes a shadowy, plump, bearded man, reminiscent of a therapist he saw some years ago. The therapist sighs as if suffering from an ache in his buttocks, swaddles down in a swivel chair, hands folded over his plump belly. He wears a dark suit and has an immaculately trimmed beard and impeccable fingernails, though he is stout, red-faced, sweaty. His voice is deep, loud, faintly theatrical. "You really have self-esteem issues, worrying about what the neighbors think. You should get some help for that. But go on. What else is on your mind?"

On this warm day in summer, he tells his therapist about his idea for the family saga, how he will recount the kidnapping of his ancestors in the frontier days and his own kidnapping. The book will be such a smashing success that it will free Jim from the clutches of President Jammer and the mad linguist, Dr. Dalton. "And there are other kidnappings as well!" he says, excitedly now. "It's all about—it's all about: where does one belong? We've all been taken—taken from our true home, and it's only a matter of getting back there! Of finding our way back home."

His therapist rolls his eyes, sighs, "If only."

Yes, yes, he will stick it to old Jammer and Dalton. Just let them try to push around a Nobel Prize winner! He won't put up with their abuse anymore! In his summer class just yesterday Jim was lecturing when the thin pale gas wafted under the door. The students paused in mid-text message, mouths agape. They all slumbered and woke in a daze. "Does anyone remember what we were talking about?" Jim asked. No one did. The students shook their heads and refocused on their text messaging.

But more importantly than his neighbors or Jammer or Dalton, his father will be impressed! The old guy doesn't get out much anymore, maybe he'll take him with him to Stockholm. Jim shuts his eyes and here's the old soldier now, back in the family kitchen, birds alighting in the bird bath way back by the alley. "Why Stockholm?" his father asks, face querulous, eyes glinty beneath his thick glasses. "Where the hell is Stockholm anyway? Europe? That's a hell of a long way to go. I don't have enough frequent flyer miles. You know if we held off until spring we might get a better deal."

"I could pay for it out of my winnings."

"It would probably be warmer in spring."

"Well, there's this thing about collecting my prize."

"What prize was that again?"

"The Nobel. The Nobel Prize."

"Oh right. What is the prize anyway? A trophy?"

"About a million bucks."

"A million bucks? That's not bad. Cash or annuity? What was it for again?"

"Our family history. Our story. Going back to the frontier days when Tom and Will got kidnapped by the Comanches. And when Len and Sis and I got kidnapped after the guy stalked Mom."

"Oh. Well, try to keep it cheerful. Nobody wants to read anything depressing. Say, if you give a little talk or something, make sure to mention your sister's a surgeon."

The O'Brien Family Saga Begins

*F*or many years, Jim's mother implored him to do justice to their family roots, to write the story of their ancestors, and he put off the project, kids, teaching, too much to take on until his dear mother was passed and gone, but now he wakes on a foggy night, parts the curtain and spies the kidnapped boys, phantoms, riding across his suburban backyard now turned to prairie. Six-year-old Will, in the year 1870, riding beside his older brother Tom, hands tied with leather straps, surrounded by six war-painted Comanches, exhausted and sore and blistered from this ride with the morning now piercing bright and hot over the plains of Texas, already many miles from home, notes with slitted eyes that he has one advantage over his eleven-year-old brother. He notes this advantage with real satisfaction. Tom has his mouth gagged but he, Will, does not. His mouth is completely free. He laughs inside at this realization. They thought Tom would cause the problems, not him. Poor Tom! Gagged! While he, Will, is free to speak! In fact, to shout! At the top of his lungs now, without Tom being able to quiet him down for once, he barks out his orders: "Let us go, you sons of bitches!"

These are six very tough Comanches surrounding the boys, and one of the places you do not want to be, one of the very places in life you do not want to be is in the clutches of the Comanches, riding north to the Staked Plains, then the canyonlands, dead man's land, where the captives are traded and separated.

But at the moment, the Comanches slow their horses and stare in wonder at the boy who keeps screaming at the top of his lungs. "TAKE US HOME NOW!" he hollers.

The Comanches stare at the hollering boy. They laugh. Then one looks angry and makes a cutting throat gesture across his own neck. But another Indian raises his hand to calm his friend. This Indian, the leader, a few years older than the others, is named White Crane, the boys will learn later, a taller, slender, dignified-looking man, who in another time and place might have been a philosopher, a poet, a physician, a diplomat, but who in fact is just a plains warrior trying to keep his little tribe intact as the Rangers and the soldiers move in closer with every year, pursuing the horse herds, raiding the camps, following them deeper into their own territory.

White Crane had counseled against taking these two boys, but they'd come across them out fishing in a creek just after dawn as the band of six were heading north after a horse raiding expedition. His rule is a loose one and he gave in to the men who wanted to take the boys, to raise them into the tribe or ransom them back later. White Crane doesn't like it, though. He knows that now the Rangers will pursue them.

White Crane takes off Tom's gag and signals the older boy to do something about his shouting younger brother. He nods at his angry friend, and Tom gets it. He needs to quiet Will down or White Crane won't be able to hold back the others.

"SONS OF BITCHES!" Will roars.

"Will," Tom says. "They're going to kill us if you don't shut up."

Will squints his eyes at Tom and gives his older brother a command. "Kill them."

"How am I supposed to kill them, Will?"

"I want to go home."

"I'm going to get us home. I promise. But you have to shut up now."

Tom has not prayed as much as he should have. His parents have always encouraged him to pray, but he mostly hasn't. He prays now. He remembers the stories of the boys who never come back, who forget where they came from, who take up with the Indians and never leave, and he vows that he will not let that happen. He will take his brother home.

"He'll shut up now," he says to White Crane, who understands the message, if not the words.

North they ride into a horrible land of rock and cactus and only the mouthfuls of stagnant water you can find in gulches, hidden draws. Bleached bones scattered about. The skin peeling from the boys' faces. The sky white with heat. Will's delirious, talking to an imaginary friend.

"Splash me!" Will chortles.

The night turns cold. They lie side by side on the ground. Tom crawls closer to Will who is struggling and stirring in his sleep and he puts his arm around his little brother and holds him through the night, and the stars come out, a great vast canopy of timeless stars, and the sound of the coyotes, and off there in the night, shuffling sounds in the sand, maybe trackers, their father, Edmund, who'd Rangered a little, though Tom's never thought of him as being all that tough, though he was a boxer back in Ireland and New York before he headed out West. He'd arrived in America a year after the Civil War, too late to fight in that, and back in the town they rode into every so often for supplies, all the hard-eyed haunted men who'd fought in that war made Edmund seem a little soft compared to them. Still, he would be out there somewhere, tracking.

They're riding again the next day and the sun is digging a hole in the top of his scalp. It's a little hole at first, a dagger hole, but it widens, and the sun fills it up. The sun fills up everything inside the hole and the hole widens. White Crane rides alongside him and throws a blanket over his head to shield him from the sun.

The Stalker

At night, in his home, there are sounds that startle Jim, and he wakes thinking of Paul Rittendorf, or Paul Roughhound, as he called him in his mind when he was a child. His wife snores, her open mouth exuding a mild, not unpleasant odor of peanut butter. He rises cautiously, to not disturb her slumbers. She's a kindly woman, but a grump if he wakes her in the night. His dog, an aging Golden Labrador with stupendous flatulence, sleeps at night in the hallway and Jim wends his way past her in the darkness, careful not to step on her tail, which would make her yelp hideously. The house was built in stages, with add-ons and doors leading haphazardly in various directions, and he sleeps fitfully, often rising to patrol the house. His wife and teenagers joke that he is watching for the Comanches. But really, he is thinking more of his own kidnapping.

Throughout the day, but most vividly late at night, scenes form in his mind and the past takes on a milky cinematic gloss, sometimes almost real, sometimes ghostly, but the scenes begin around 1960, when he is five.

A family starting out on the north side of San Antonio, on just cleared land, the rattlesnakes making a last stand. Only yesterday evening, Danny O'Brien, a Marine who'd battled in the Philippines, was ringed suddenly by two rattlers, hissing and snapping at him in the far corner of the lot where a new garden and birdbath try to tame the surrounding shrubbery. "Honey!" he yelled, "throw me a golf club!" And Jim's mother flew out of the garage, dark hair askew, eyes wild and primed and tossed the club, a five iron, to Danny, who wound up and swung, but duffed the shot, whacking the club head into the dirt. Still, the snakes wiggled hell-bent for the alley. Danny's face was flushed. "Never a dull moment around here!"

Jim's mother put a hand to her mouth. "The kids," she said hoarsely. "How can we leave the kids out here?"

But Len, eleven, Jim's older brother, whisked out the sliding glass door with his pump-action BB rifle. "I'll get 'em," he said.

"Whoa now, son. They've learned their lesson. Rattlers aren't stupid. They don't want to mess with a crew like us."

That was yesterday, and this morning five-year-old Jim O'Brien digs himself deep under his sheets because he is scheduled to go off to kindergarten for the first day.

He will not move. He will sink lower and lower into his sheets until he disappears. They will go off and forget him here, in the lower bunk bed. But a crazed snorting creature, hairy-chested, wearing white underwear, appears at the foot of the bed, bellowing, "Rise and shine, Sunshine!" His father grins monstrously, grips him by the ankles and pulls, and Jim's fingers claw at the sheets, dragging them along as his father dumps him on the floor.

He hears the name for the first time at the breakfast table. "Paul Rittendorf," his father muses, looking out at the far side of the backyard, an area mostly uncleared of brush, but containing a white birdbath, rising like a relic in a jungle. "Why would Paul Rittendorf call here? He was a weirdo even back then."

"I know he was," Jim's mother says.

"Why would he call here?" But then movement distracts Jim's father. "Look! Two birds are drinking from the birdbath." There is a sad yet happy lilt to his voice. "Is this the first time they've come?"

Jim looks up from his cereal, milk smeared across his lips. "No. Len shot one yesterday. He shot it and it fell in the water and we threw it in the alley for the spray cats to eat."

His father's mouth hangs open as he stares at the birdbath. "Well, there you go."

"He killed it?" his mother asks. "He killed the poor bird?"

"For the spray cats to eat."

"The stray cats, love."

Len comes into the kitchen. "I was just practicing. I didn't think I'd hit it."

"Let the birds drink in peace, will you?" their father says. "How'd you like it if someone shot at you every time you tried to get a drink?"

Len's tongue works against the side of his mouth. "I guess I wouldn't like it."

"Last night," Sis says. She is seven and they all look at her because she is always saying things that shake them up, as if she's in touch with strange, menacing forces. "I saw a light."

Their mother's eyes narrow in on her. "What light, Sis?"

"It shined in my window. Then it was gone."

"What kind of a light?"

"It came in the window. Then it was gone. I don't know." She stares at her milk and her lips tighten. That's all they're getting out of her. Jim can picture her in movies, being questioned by the enemy, bright lights shined in her face. She gives her captors nothing.

By the time they are driving to school, the name Paul Rittendorf has turned in his mind to Paul Roughhound, and Paul Roughhound has merged in his mind with the light shining in Sis's window. The light heralds a new trouble in their lives. But there is not much time to think of this now because his mother has pulled into the long circular driveway of the convent school and a nun with hairs sprouting from a vast mole throws open the back door and grins with broken teeth. "Hello, child," she says. He screams and grabs hold of the inner door handle and Sis's arm as the nun tries to drag him out. As he holds on to both Sis and the handle, the rest of the blackrobes move in. They stretch him out like a rope, two pulling at his feet, two prying at his fingers, one pinching the nerve between his shoulder and neck. Len and Sis, who must be driven along to their own school, eye him darkly, contemptuously, as his fingers slip away. His mother's eyes well up with tears. "Jim, I explained all this," she soothes. Certainly she *explained* it. But he never *agreed!*

He reaches a supplicating hand out to Sis, his elder by two years and an eternity of wisdom, his sister, the veritable soul of understanding and consolation, his Sis, as pure and kind as the Blessed Mother herself. Ah, blessed Sis. She shirks back from him as if to avoid a beseeching leper. She raises her foot and grinds the white sole of her St. Theresa of the Little Flower school shoe against his nose and kicks him out the door. As he wails, the nuns cart him off like a battering ram.

⌒⌒⌒

Evening in the backyard.

"You see this, kids," their father says. He picks up a white dirt clod from the earth. He's still wearing his work shirt. Tie loose a notch. Jaunty looking. Rough, handsome face. Large nose off center.

"This is colichee," he says, kneading the clod in his hand.

"Colichee," Jim says, working the sound around on his tongue.

"That's right. *Col-eech-ee.* This is the stuff we got to get rid of if our grass is going to grow. Every time you see it, pick it up and throw it into the alley."

"I want my own bathroom," Sis says. "They whiz all over the toilet."

"Why don't you boys aim a little better?" He kisses the top of her head, gathers them all in, hugs them. "I wish I had more nights when I got home early like this."

He goes in to change clothes after work, and Momma comes out to throw the softball. Jim stands waggling the bat while she calls in her drawl, "Swing, honey, swing!" The ball looms before his eyes, wide and white and dropping through the twilight. But he does not swing. He's waiting for the perfect pitch, the pitch that he can hammer over Momma's head, over Len's leaping glove, over the fence, high above the neighbors' roofs, into orbit, up to the moon's drooping eyes watching over them all here in the gathering dusk of summer in this Alamo city of siege and cannon fire, where city meets country, where the O'Briens, settlers, stalwarts, do battle with the rattlesnakes and the bandits and Comanches that ride out of the hills every full moon to raid and sack the ranch.

Then later, after they're fed, after the baby's been put to bed and the backyard has fallen into darkness, his mother and father smoke on the patio, their cigarettes glowing red in the night. As Len and Sis swoop around in the yard, Len chasing, Sis shrieking in delight, Jim comes in like a spy, a spook, an infiltrator, lies flat on the soil and the sprigs of grass trying to spurt their way through the colichee, lies there and listens as his father says, "I'm not going to get mad. I'm just trying to figure out what's going on here and if we've got something to worry about. Just tell me what happened."

"It was such a long time ago. I hadn't talked to him since then until he called a few days ago." Ice tinkles in their drinks and the cigarettes glow brighter, like fireflies. "He got a wound in his arm," she says. "So he came back early from the war."

"I see."

"What do you mean you see? It's not like what you're thinking."

"I don't know what I'm thinking. I'm all shook up. Go on."

"He came into the drugstore a couple of times. He wanted someone to talk to."

"What did you talk about?"

"Nothing much. High school. The old football games. He talked about the way you played quarterback."

"He couldn't catch worth a lick. So what happened?"

"His Momma died. She'd been sick a long time. His Daddy had died when he was little and he didn't have much family, so I thought I ought to go to the funeral. Betty came along. At the cemetery, he asked if I'd come to his house for the wake. He looked so lonely, I said okay."

"You went to his house?"

"I went with Betty. People were drinking. Before I knew it, Betty went off and left me, and when I said I was going, he said he'd give me a ride home."

"This is too much."

Her voice breaks. "I'm trying to get it all out so you'll know. I've saved this up inside for a lot of years."

The ice tinkles in his glass. "Go on."

"We started to drive. I thought he was driving me home, but then he started making turns and he said he wanted to show me something. Right then I knew something was wrong with him."

"My God."

"He was driving too fast for me to jump out. He drove us out to the country. Out to some land that his family owned, out in the sticks. Somewhere around New Braunfels. There was nothing out there but an old cabin.

"He walked me around the land. There wasn't much. Mesquite trees, cactus, rocks. It was starting to get dark. We sat on the edge of the porch, on the planks. There weren't even any chairs. He had a flask and he kept trying to get me to take a drink, but I wouldn't. He was drunk. But it wasn't the way people usually get when they're drunk. He wasn't sloppy or slurring. It was more like he wasn't really there.

"I asked him to take me home, and he just shook his head and said he didn't know. It was scary, the way he said it, like he didn't know himself if he was going to take me home. He kept getting madder and madder, but it wasn't like how people usually get mad. He never even raised his voice, and that made me even more scared. I had a rock hidden in my hand and I was about to hit him when he asked if I was crying. I guess I was. I guess I was crying. I told him my parents would be worried about me.

"He said he didn't have any parents now. He said all his people were dead and his mother was a crazy old bitch. I told him I always thought that she was nice. And he started crying and saying, 'I'm sorry, Momma, I'm sorry I called you a crazy old bitch.' He kind of crumpled over and cried on me.

"Then he got up and said let's go. Get in the car. I didn't say anything. I knew it would go bad somehow if I said anything. I leaned as far against the car door as I could all the way home, ready to jump if he got crazy again. Then outside my house, he said he wanted to see me again. He tried to kiss me and I jumped out and ran . . .

"His car would come by sometimes without stopping. Sometimes the phone would ring and there'd be nobody there. But he never came into the drugstore anymore. I heard he'd moved away. Then I heard he was in prison for armed robbery. Then I got the call last week . . . He said he wanted to check on me. He said he wanted to make sure I was being treated all right. He . . . he asked about the kids."

Jim's father's cigarette glows in the darkness. "If he comes around here . . ."

"Don't do something crazy," Jim's mother says. "This will pass. He'll drift on."

She begins to cry. "I thought it was all over. I just want him to go away."

❧

One evening coming back from the playground, Len riding behind on his bike, Jim and Sis walking a little ahead, a white poodle dashes out of a house and across the street with two kids in chase, yelling, "Come back, Scruffy!" On his bike, Len goes after the escaping pooch. Swooping down like a cowboy snatching a senorita off the street, he snags the dog in one hand as Jim and Sis and the two other little kids cheer.

A battered old car screeches to a stop beside them. A pirate jumps out. Silver tooth in front, stubbly-cheeked, ropy-veined Popeye forearms, dirty white T-shirt, blue jeans, cowboy boots. The pirate snatches Jim with one steely hand and Sis with the other, and as they shriek, he tosses them into the back seat and swings the door shut. As Roughhound tries to go in the driver's door, Len drops Scruffy at the feet of the two neighborhood children, then charges in on his high-handle-bar bicycle and dives onto Roughhound's neck. Roughhound grabs him by the hair and throws him into the front seat.

Roughhound speeds away. Looking back through the rear window Jim sees the two neighborhood children holding the white poodle, waving as the car turns the corner. Len's on his back, kicking his feet at Roughhound's side and Roughhound snarls, "You keep that up and I'll break your foot for you." Sis leans over the seat and says, "Don't fight him now, Len. I'll kill him later with a pin."

Roughhound glances wide-eyed over the seat at her, his brow sweaty.

She is talking now to Jim, in the back seat, "I take the pin. Behind his ear. One little move. One little touch and he's dead. Dead," she grunts, her eyes hollowing out, her voice spooky, from the depths, and Jim sees them in a dark bead-curtained room, Sis dancing like an Egyptian, her belly bare, her wrists bejeweled, Roughhound reclining on a big pillow as Sis dances nearer and inserts the pin behind his ear. "Dead," she moans, transported zombie dancer from an old movie or something, "Dead. Dead . . . "

"Shut that little girl up!" Roughhound shouts.

They turn corners and go faster and faster, the kids in the back swaying from side to side, bouncing off doors, Len lying in the front, quiet for a moment, but then he springs back into action, releases another barrage of kicks at Roughhound. This time Roughhound one-hands the steering wheel, reaches out and grabs Len by the waist of his jeans, pulls Len in closer, sliding him down the seat toward him as Len wiggles and kicks at him. Roughhound works him closer until he can grab Len by the throat. He chokes until Len lets out a squelchy sucking sound and then he releases and Len lies there coughing and holding his throat.

"You kids settle down," Roughhound says. "I ain't going to hurt you."

They're barreling now into ranch lands and hills. He presses the accelerator down, down, and Jim holds Sis's hand as they sink against each other in the seats that smell of something old and foul and rancid.

Down rough dirt roads. Roughhound freewheels and jimmies the battered car up to an old plank and hack board cabin and parks beside a broken, lopsided porch.

He hops out, opens the back door, flashing his silver tooth. "Mi casa, su casa."

Len gets out from the front seat and moves fast around the car so that he can guard Jim and Sis when they struggle from the car, blinking in the evening glare as Roughhound beams at all three. "Don't be shy now, kids. We're going to have us a right good time."

"Why are you doing this?" Len demands.

Roughhand scratches his stubbly cheek. "Why? You ask your Momma why. I told her to meet me once, just once. Now she'll have to meet me, won't she?"

His eyes soften and cloud over. "We're all going to be a family," he says tearfully.

"He's crazy!" Len screams. "Run!"

But Roughhound grabs hold of Jim's arm. "You coming inside, boy?"

He gives Jim's arm a tug and Jim cries out in pain, and Len says, "Okay, mister, okay." They go into the cabin and Roughhound kicks the door shut. The cabin is dim in the evening light. Keeping himself between them and the door, Roughhound lights a propane lantern. There's one main room with a brick fireplace, a roughed out kitchen in one corner, a small bedroom off the main room. A couple of straight-backed chairs and a heavy wooden rectangular table. Roughhound stands guarding the door. "All right," he says. "I'm going to tell you the truth now." He pauses, gulps air, voice coming out strangled. "I'm your real father."

Sis sinks to her knees on the plankboards. She bends over and dry heaves.

"You're a liar," Len says.

Roughhound stares sadly at him. "You were always the tough one."

"You're not our father. You're making that up because you're crazy."

Roughhound stares at him, his tongue working at a sore tooth. "That's the second time you've called me that. My word, you're an unpleasant bunch of children."

Roughhound's face turns dark. He looks about to rush at them, but then the air sags out of him. He leans back against the door. His back slowly slides down it until he's sitting on the floor. He shuts his eyes. With his knees up, he lowers his head to his hands. "You kids all sit for a minute," he says groggily.

Len leads them over by the fireplace and pulls over the two chairs. He has them sit, while he stands, watching Roughhound.

After a couple of minutes, Roughhound, eyes still closed, calls out, "Hey, tough kid. Listen to me. Go in the kitchen. On the table there, there's some mugs and a jug of water. You pour a cup for your brother and sister. And yourself. You pour yourself a cup, too."

Len doesn't say anything, but he goes to the table. Jim sees him slide something into the waistband of his jeans and cover it with his shirt. He pours the water and they drink thirstily. Without looking up, Roughhound says, "On that table, there's two bottles of pills. Now you get me some of those pills and you get me my water now, too. Okay? Will you do that for me, tough kid?" he says, but he says it in a quiet, almost nice voice.

"Okay," Len says. He goes to the table. "How many pills you want?"

"It don't matter exactly. A good handful. I got a real bad headache."

Len pours pills from both bottles into the palm of his hand and brings Roughhound the pills and a cup of water.

Without looking up at him, Roughhound opens his palm and Len pours the pills into the center of his hand. Roughhound raises his hand and drops all the pills into his mouth at once and washes them down with big swallows of water. Still with his eyes shut, he jiggles the cup. "A little more water."

Len brings him the water and backs away without turning his eyes, all the time watching Roughhound.

Roughhound's eyes lift up and pop open and it's almost enough to make Jim fall out of his chair. Roughhound stands up, flashing his silver-toothed grin. "That's what's missing. I needed to think of something fun to do." He opens the door and Jim sees there's still a little sunlight left. "Come on out on the porch."

As Len passes by, Roughhound says, "Don't run, tough kid. I can catch at least one of them."

He gestures toward the edge of the porch. "You kids sit here. I got a real nice surprise for you." He walks out to a burned-out brick fire pit. He finds an old smashed up tin can, and he sets it in place on the fire pit wall. He flashes the silver tooth.

"Crazier than shit," Len whispers.

Roughhound freezes with his hand on the can. "Did you say something?"

Len shakes his head. "Nope."

Jim slips his hand into Len's. It's been a while since he's slipped his hand into Len's, but Len squeezes it, holds it tight.

"What are you doing?" Len asks Roughhound, but he takes the edge from his voice.

Roughhound's mouth plays around like it's trying to find the right position, to give or to take or to scold, but his lips soften and loosen and twist back into a grin as he walks back past them into the cabin, and he comes out a moment later carrying a small flat box and dragging one of the old wooden chairs with him. He pauses for a second, setting the box on the seat of the chair. "What's that girl doing?"

They look over at Sis. She's kneeling a few feet away from them on the porch and making the sign of the cross, touching her head, the center of her flat chest, her left shoulder, her right.

"She's praying," Len says. "She's pretty religious."

Roughhound squats down in front of her. "Little girl?"

She continues making the sign of the cross until he grabs her hands.

"What are you praying for, little girl?"

Her eyes open a slit, and she offers him an angelic smile. "For your soul at the moment of your death."

He rocks back on the heels of his cowboy boots.

"What's in the box, mister?" Len asks.

Roughhound gives Sis a long look, but he stands up and moves to the box on the chair. He opens the box and reveals a long barreled pistol.

"German," Roughhound says.

Len whistles. "It's a beauty."

Roughhound laughs. "It's just a pellet gun," he says.

"I knew that."

Roughhound laughs louder, sounding like a kid on the play-ground who's pulled off a good trick. "You didn't neither."

"I did."

"Naw, you did not. You did not. You admit it now." Still laugh-ing, a great horsy laugh, he takes hold of Len's arm and twists it behind his back until Len winces. "Admit it, now, you admit it. Go on."

Jim touches Len's leg, signaling him to answer. "I admit it," Len says in a tight voice, and Jim knows that if it were just Len there he'd never admit it, never admit it even if Roughhound broke his arm.

Roughhound releases his arm and gives a laugh. "Got you that time!"

Len shakes his head. "You sure did."

Roughhound removes a silver pellet from a small red tin can and loads the gun. He goes to one knee, using the arm of the chair as a brace. He takes aim at the can, squeezes the trig-ger, and the pellet whizzes out in the high grasses somewhere behind the firepit. "I nicked it," Roughhound says.

He loads another pellet and hands the gun to Len, who holds the gun out with a straight arm, squinting an eye.

"Naw, that ain't the right way," Roughhound says. "You need a brace for your shooting arm."

Len squeezes off the shot and the can spins off the brick wall.

Roughhound blows air out of his mouth. "Dumb luck," he says. But then he laughs. "Double or nothing. Like to see you do that again."

He loads the gun for Len again, then Roughhound walks out to the fire pit. He grins, sets the can back up, stands off to the side a little. "Try it again."

Len fires and the can just sits there. Roughhound laughs.

"Told you it was luck."

Len loads as Roughhound starts walking back to them. "Hey, I didn't tell you you could load."

"Sorry," Len says. When Roughhound is five feet from them, Len raises the gun and fires into the center of his face.

Roughhound screams and falls backwards, clutching at his head. "Run!" Len commands them, and they scamper from the porch and bolt off below the now darkening sky.

Roughhound shouts, "You want to play guns?"

He goes inside the cabin to a chest and comes out with the .357 Magnum. "I'll play guns you little sons of bitches!" he cries, firing into the sky.

Len pulls them along through the brush, leading them away from the dirt road, figuring Roughhound will expect them to head that way. Their friend is the coming darkness. "Keep going," he orders Jim and Sis. He breaks away from them, running back toward the road but staying hidden in the brush, making as much noise as he can so Roughhound will follow him away from Len and Sis. He stoops down, picks up a rock and hurls it far ahead and he hears Roughhound's footsteps run in that direction.

Roughhound chases after the sound but then he whirls about. Those young punks aren't heading toward the road. Trying to fool him. They sure are, they sure are. They got gumption, though, he'll give them credit for that. He sort of wishes they really were his kids. Danny doesn't deserve this crew. Danny got all the credit back in high school. Quarterback, my ass, couldn't throw worth a shit! Fucking war hero. Hero. Bullshit. Does a guy get any credit? Crawling up that goddamn hill and the bullets whizzing through the grass and looking over and seeing Big Lou with a hole in his head, still climbing. He climbed another three feet on his belly with that hole in his head before he knew he was dead. That was the thing that got me. I think I was all right until then. It was looking over at Big Lou and realizing he was dead and still crawling. I screamed then. I screamed and ran at the bastards and then I pitched the grenade and came in firing and cleared out the bunker and then the next bunker of guys came out with their hands up as if they knew I was coming, as if the word had spread that old Paul Rittendorf himself was charging the whole goddamn hill by himself. They came out and threw up their hands and I shot them and stuck the fuckers with the bayonet . . . Surrender? Fuck you! Does a guy get any credit?

❦

Jim steps on a cactus and the sharp points penetrate his tennis shoe. He hops a few feet, then sits down on the ground.

Sis stands above him. "Get on my back."

She carries Jim, bouncing him along.

They hear Roughhound crashing through the brush. Sis tries to run faster. Then she's not going anywhere, running in place as Roughhound holds onto Jim's belt. "Gotcha!" Roughhound says. Jim pitches off Sis's back, falls to the ground, and Sis runs at Roughhound, punching at his groin and yelling, "Run, Jim!" He crawls into the brush, but Roughhound smacks Sis down with his hand and then he grabs her up by her hair. "You better come out, kid. I got your sister. I'm going to tug on her hair a little bit here . . . " Sis screams and Jim comes out of the brush. Roughhound hauls him in, throwing him over his shoulder and carting him off like a sack of wheat, as Sis follows, beating at his back. He knocks her down. "One kid will do," he says. "You're all starting to get on my nerves." He looks around. "Where's the tough kid? Hey, tough kid," he calls into the brush. "You ain't so tough, are you? Scared to help your little brother. You see that, kid, he's scared to help you."

He carries Jim back to the cabin. He throws him into the front seat of the car. "Stay put."

He goes inside the cabin and as he's coming back out with his arms loaded up, a shadowy figure in a white T-shirt steps onto the porch, and plunges something into his thigh. Roughhound screams and staggers, clutching at his thigh, the knife buried in it.

Len runs to the car and Sis hops into the back seat. Len turns the key in the ignition and steps on the gas, sending Sis flying against the front seat and Jim slamming into the dashboard. "You don't know how to drive!" Sis screams.

Roughhound staggers after the car, weaving in a strange lop-sided run in the moonlight. He fires the gun as the car bounces ahead over the rocky pitted road, rounds a bend and leaves him behind.

The windows are down, the wind sails through their hair, the car cuts down the narrow dirt road as Len's hands hold steady on the steering wheel, his face set tight and grim and resolute. He says quietly, "Everybody all right?"

They bounce on, and by the time they hit the paved road, Len seems like he's been driving for years, didn't just learn it from watching their father. They see the lights of a country store up ahead, but Len says, "I'm not stopping at the first place, just in case. Let's keep moving a little down the road."

And for a little while, Jim thinks they're setting out on their own, Len and Sis and him, and he's okay with that, if Len is there. But at the next lighted store, Len stops the car. Before he goes inside to call the police and their parents, he puts his hands to his face, and Jim sees that Len's shoulders are shaking. "Stay here," Len says, but they won't. As he opens his door, they're already following him into a warm, moonlit night in the country.

Out on the Lone Prairie

The hard winter sets into the high canyonlands. Will and Tom hunker down in a wickiup out near the horses, barely alive, burrowing against one another for warmth. Will's developed a cough. He spits up blood. Tom wakes with a startled scream as a terrible painted face hovers over them.

But White Crane's paint is not the paint of war, but of grief. He has lost his family to the plague. Lost his wife, lost his wife and precious son. He is alone, the most alone man in the world, and he wears the savage face of lamentation, a hideous clown's face of woe.

The wild tear-streaked face hovers above the boys. With his knife he lashes, not the boys, but his own ear. He hands a bloody hunk of ear to Tom, who whispers, "No thanks. I don't want your ear."

White Crane closes the boy's hand over the bloody hunk of ear. He speaks no English, but Tom understands him.

Take my ear, he says.

"All right, thanks," Tom says.

White Crane disappears into the vast, dark night. The boys

hear him off wailing beneath the half-moon.

He sleeps again and when he wakes up, he and Will have been covered in warm buffalo skins.

A day, a night, another sleep. In his sleep, Tom feels himself lifted by strong arms. He imagines that it is father, Edmund, the happy singing man with the strong arms who would throw him up in the top bunk at bedtime, giving him the "fisherman's toss," as they called it.

But it is White Crane, carrying him into his tipi. He puts Tom down amidst soft hides and furs. A small fire glows in the center of the tipi, the smoke carried toward a hole in the top.

Warmth. Delicious, wonderful warmth.

White Crane takes his own place across the tipi, grunts, lies down, as if something is settled. Tom is home. He is no longer prisoner now, no longer slave. White Crane is his father now. He is family. White Crane's son. A member of the tribe.

He yearns to stay in that warmth. But he rises, crawls toward the flap opening in the tipi.

White Crane rises to an elbow. What are you doing? Tom knows he's asking.

"I'm going back to my brother."

White Crane shakes his head and Tom knows he is saying: Too late. He'll die. He unties the sash. White Crane jumps up, pulls him away from the opening. He lies in bed until he hears White Crane's steady snores.

His feet trail blood all the way to the wickiup. He staggers through blowing snow and howling wind. He lies down beside Will, snuggles into him, covers the barely breathing boy with his own body, breathes his own breath against Will's chest. He shuts his eyes, says the prayer of death, asks God to take them into His home.

In his sleep, he's being lifted again under one strong arm and as his eyelids flutter, he realizes White Crane is carrying something under the other arm. He carries the boys back to the tipi, drops them side by side on the soft furs. White Crane looks at Will, at the blood seeping from his mouth, and he lets out a yelp of despair, disappears through the opening, going back in the frigid night.

A few minutes later he slips back into the tipi, followed by an ancient-looking woman, an old crone with dried, wrinkled skin. Over the fire she brews a foul-smelling concoction. Pours some steaming fluid into a hide cup. Kneels over Will. Puts a gnarled hand under his neck, lifts his head. Presses the cup to his lips.

"Get that out of here," Will mutters, eyes closed.

"Drink," she coaxes.

"No," Will says. An absolute no. A *no* that bears no hint of *yes*. No. Will's *no*.

Tom knows the woman doesn't speak English, but he tries to explain about Will. "There isn't any use talking to him. We'll have to tie him down."

But she tries again, tilting the cup, raising his head a few inches. Will left hooks the cup out of her hand. The hot liquid flies through the air and spatters White Crane.

The old woman laughs. She looks at Tom and speaks in the Comanche tongue. He seems to understand her. "Your brother is a crazy wild man," she says.

"Sorry. He's always been that way."

With his eyes closed, Will says, "I'll kill you."

She laughs. "He might live," she says.

She goes out in the darkness. White Crane sticks his head out of the tipi, calls in a wailing voice, but she does not come back.

She's left some of the concoction. Tom pins Will's arms and

White Crane holds Will's chin, lifts the cup to his lips as Will bites at the air like a rabid dog.

White Crane gentles the hot liquid into him, sip by sip. He holds his hand over Will's mouth to keep the foul brew in, howls once and jumps back as Will bites his hand. But he resumes, more careful now, pouring the liquid in sip by sip as Tom holds Will's struggling arms.

When they are through forcing the brew into him, they step back. Tom prays, and he hears White Crane chanting softly, and he realizes White Crane is praying in his own way.

The wild Indian prays over his brother. He should never have taken them, and Tom reminds himself to hate the Indian, but he listens to White Crane chanting and he has to force the hatred up. He cannot let himself forget the hatred. He must hear his mother reading to them at night, hear his father's singing voice, feel the lift of his real father's arms giving him the fisherman's toss.

White Crane rubs Will's face, his arms, his legs, his chest. Rubs to bring the life back. He cries as if Will is his son now, too, made his son the moment he carried him into the tipi.

In the morning, Will's fever is broken and his cough is better. He keeps getting better. The winter snows melt away, and spring comes beautifully on the high plains. They are White Crane's children now, members of the tribe, and the children love the tricks they know—the boxing and wrestling and gymnastics Edmund had taught them. Will can stand on his hands and walk around the entire camp as they cheer. He can do back-handed flips and land on his feet. The children have never really seen boxing. They marvel as Tom patters them about the head and stomach.

The years go by and they live as wild Indians. Tom fights it inside, clings to the pictures of home, but Will's letting it go. What good is the past to him now? What good are his parents? They never came for him. He cannot even see their faces anymore. They are part of an old dream, and soon he will lose even the dream. Tom fights for him, reminds him of the old days, but Will runs from him or covers his ears. He does not even like the old language anymore. He refuses to understand it. But inside Tom has not forgotten his promise. He will take Will home.

Of Quilting Shows and Counseling

*I*n the makeshift room above their garage, Jim lies on the old couch as dust motes drift in the sunlight, and appearing through a glint of light, the therapist sighs, arranges one thick buttock in the swivel chair, crooks his torso, settles in the other thick buttock. He folds his hands over his plump belly. "So," he says in his stentorian voice, "what do you have for me today?"

"I wake up all night long, imagining someone breaking into my house. I guess it's not all that unusual. I was kidnapped as a child and I guess that had a damaging effect on me."

The therapist clears his throat. "Are you a trained therapist?"

"Why, no."

"Then why would you leap to the conclusion that the kidnapping damaged you in some way? Doesn't that strike you as a flimsy excuse? People go through much worse things all the time."

"I suppose so."

"Repeat after me: *I was kidnapped as a child.*"

"I was kidnapped as a child."

"Okay. Now how did you feel, saying that?"

"I felt a little sad."

"Sad? You got away, didn't you? Case closed."

"And a few years after Roughhound, there was the Major."

"The Major?"

"A child molester."

"Oh my God," he mutters. "Next you're going to be telling me that boring story as well." He rubs his head. "I don't think I can stand this. Let's change the subject. Tell me about that golf quilt again."

Jim sighs, but recounts the last summer's vacation from the college. In a sleepy town in Oregon, Jim's wife forces him to go with her to a quilting show at the Town Hall, which serves as a combination central meeting place and the fire station. A long time ago, when they were first married, he served as a volunteer fire fighter. When the siren went off, he'd boldly throw down his dinner fork. They had an unreliable car in those days, so he'd leap a wooden fence and sprint a half mile across a meadow to arrive panting at the station, ready to strap on the heavy yellow jacket. He dreamed of coming home to tell his wife how he'd dragged someone out of a burning home, but many of the fires involved uninhabited dwellings. He was mostly relegated to the inglorious role of "broom man," where he would sweep up ash after a fire. He was relieved when a more professional crew took over the firehouse and released the volunteers from service.

The quilting show is not the sort of thing he goes to willingly, but they are visiting relatives in this bucolic town in Oregon and attendance at the Fourth of July weekend quilting show is a requirement. He survives the annual ritual by imagining Comanches laying siege to the Town Hall. His wife even makes their two teenage boys attend. But there is a payoff. They know, from previous years, that once they pass through the quilting show in the front of the Town Hall, they will come to the pancake and bacon breakfast. The boys speed through the hanging quilts at a dead run and arrive safely at the pancake table.

Jim is not so lucky, though. His wife captures his arm and makes him walk beside her as they study each quilt hanging from the rafters. His wife envisions buying one for their bedroom at home, solicits his opinions. He is neutral about their aesthetic appeal, mostly checks price tags, shakes his head no. As his stomach growls, he wonders what's taking the Comanches so long to strike. But then he draws up with a sudden stop, eyes widening in awe. There are squares in the quilt and in each square there's a man golfing. In each square, he's in progressive stages of his swing. How glorious is the quilted little golfer's swing! The sunlight beams on the quilt.

The therapist works his thick buttocks around on the chair. "Here, get up. Show me the swing. Slowly now."

Jim stands. He addresses the imaginary ball, starts a slow backswing, emulating the quilted golfer.

"That's nice," the therapist says. "That's very nice."

With a sigh, the therapist assumes his own comfy position on the couch. He folds his trimmed fingernails over his belly. "The wrist, arm alignment, the tuck of the chin. The quilt captured all that?"

The therapist closes his eyes. "Okay, Jim, here's the deal. I'm willing to listen from time to time, I'll take as much as I can, but when I can't take any more there will be silence. Do you understand? All right, so you have a problem with this childhood thing. You yourself were kidnapped. And you had two ancestors who were kidnapped by the Comanches, and you worry constantly about your own children."

"I wouldn't say *constantly*."

"Who asked your opinion? Now, I'm going to snooze for a little here while you tell me about your own children's lives. Generalities will do. Personally, I find childhood most uninteresting."

He dozes off as Jim talks about his own children. He recalls football and baseball seasons, swimming lessons, Happy Meals, gymnastics.

"Boring," his therapist intones from the couch in a groggy voice. He tells him of the time one of them asked if there were a frog in heaven, the reply being that perhaps there might be room for a frog in heaven, when it was revealed he had said *fog*. Was there a fog in heaven? He tells him of the way their high-pitched voices were like a serenade to him, before the voices changed, grew deep as they turned into young men. Tells him of the way that one could swing back and forth on the monkey bars for a half an hour or the way another made a thousand bounces on the trampoline, counting them out one by one and making him count along.

Probably, he hovered over them too much. Checked too many doors and windows in the night.

The family read, the family sang. It wasn't all happiness. He yelled sometimes. Who knows how much damage is done, but they are in their teen years now, and it is a new ballgame, one he can hardly keep up with. He feels like a volunteer firefighter, arrived windblown and helpless to meet their new needs.

In Which the Therapist Demands to Talk About Sex

The therapist groans and snorts a white powder from a vial. "Cut to the chase already," the therapist croaks. "Go back to your own pathetic teen years. Get to that Cicely broad again. Give me some sex, something I can sink my teeth into. Go on. I'll just lie here and have a sniff from time to time. No worries."

Jim, thirteen, lies in bed. Lower bunk. Late at night. Wakes and hears no comforting sounds from upper bunk—no heavy breathing, no sighs, no stirrings in dreams. He prays for Len's safe return.

Len's got too much energy to contain. He drinks to tamp down the energy, to keep it from overloading him. He drives the back roads with his friends. They go out drinking and shooting and hollering. Sometimes he takes off on his friends. They go out camping and Len picks up a backpack and disappears in the brush country, and Jim thinks he's out there looking for Roughhound, who escaped and was never found. Jim knows Len's gearing up for something. Len's getting ready for some mission, steeling himself, and Jim just wants him back in the top bunk.

The voices of his parents drift down the hallway from the kitchen where they're having a late-night snack, staring in worry at the 2:00 a.m. on the clock.

"I don't get it," Jim's father says. "He was always such a good kid. I mean, a little wild, but a good kid."

"He still is a good kid," Jim's mother says.

"Kids are all weird as hell these days. Ever since the Beatles. Why the hell didn't they stay in England where they belonged?"

"Get to the Cicely broad," the therapist says sleepily. "I like the sexy stuff."

Jim sits at the kitchen table waiting for the call from Cicely that will signal her mother has left the house. She's been grounded again, so it's the only way he can see her. After her mother's left, Jim will run there—it's a mile, mostly uphill, and from the moment he hops up from the table, he'll slip through her back door in seven minutes, though on the downhill coming home, he'll crack six minutes. He's been getting in good shape this summer, making the run to Cicely's.

He's playing Monopoly with Sis and his mother and his two younger brothers and he almost wishes the call would not come.

It's such a warm, languid, innocent morning playing Monopoly at the kitchen table, and he's cozy and home and feeling like a kid again, and he hardly understands this strange world he's entered with Cicely, and he wishes it were like the old days, with Len still living at home, not in the Marines, not fighting in a war far away, and all of them out on a summer evening with Momma slow pitching the softball and calling, "Swing, honey, swing!"

Sis covets Boardwalk. Seventeen years old now and she covets Boardwalk. A blonde now. She has shocked them all by dyeing her hair. In a few moments, she will trade toughly but fairly for

Boardwalk and soon drive them all out of the game, including the youngest, Dan, who has been building hotels on property he doesn't own. But the call comes from Cicely. Two rings and then silence. His mother stares at the phone.

He starts to sweat. He waits three minutes so it will not be obvious and then he springs up, blurts, "I'll be right back. I forgot something at the reservoir!"

His mother gives him the dark-eye and Sis shouts, "You can't leave. I just got Boardwalk!"

As he bolts out the front door, invisible fingers seem to reach at him to try to draw him back to that kitchen table in the morning sunlight, and maybe if he'd let the invisible fingers pull him back to that table in the sun, Momma cooking and Sis coveting nothing more than Boardwalk, all would have been different somehow, ended differently, ended happily. But the fingers clutch and release; he breaks from them, he is running, he is always running.

From the couch, the therapist stirs, his eyes opening wide. "That isn't bad, really. Not a bad metaphor in a sense. Running. Invisible fingers. But if only you would let the invisible fingers pull you back . . . What does it all mean to you? Not that I really care about your opinion."

"Actually, they're not entirely invisible, it occurs to me."

"No?"

"The fingers are like bands of light, or rays, blue and red and yellow rays stretching out, and they're almost leaving smudges on my white T-shirt."

"Your mother's fingers?"

"I suppose . . . It's as if in that moment, life could have turned one way or the other."

"Why would that have affected Len?"

"I don't know. I feel like I set off some bad luck somehow. Or maybe if I had been drawn back, he would have been drawn back, too. We would have all ended up back there together again."

"Go on. Get to the sex."

He runs up the hill, past the grassy enclosure behind the water reservoir, down an alleyway, backyard dogs barking savagely. Springs over Cicely's chain link fence. Old mangy Jeeter nips at his jeans, but he's too fast for Jeeter. Sprints across the backyard, slips into the den through the patio's sliding glass door.

And there is splendid Cicely. Standing in front of the living room couch, she opens her terrycloth robe, naked beneath. Perfectly naked. Perfectly slender. A sculptor's finely drawn curves within the dancer's flat build, so much fine mystery on such a tiny frame. Still damp from her bath.

It takes him three seconds to unbuckle and slide down his jeans to his knees and they fall down on the couch, with her already leading him in, sliding him into a silky moist warm velveteen world. Thirty-one seconds after he's entered the house, seven minutes and three seconds after he jumped up from the kitchen table, he cries out, "Yow!"

She wraps her legs around him, savors him for five seconds more, then pushes on his chest and orders, "Go! She'll be back in a minute!"

Jeans up and zipped, and less than a minute after entering the house, he's back out the sliding glass door and running across the backyard, Jeeter attached to his ankle. He shakes off the cranky old dog at the top of the fence. Runs back up the alleyway, crosses behind the reservoir and drops down the hill to home and thirteen and a half minutes after he jumped up from the table, he's sitting back down, his head covered in sweat.

He holds up the watch that was hidden in his pocket. "I left my watch at the reservoir yesterday when we were playing football. I remembered I had to get it." He dangles the watch for them to see.

His mother gives him the evil eye again. "Who was that on the phone?"

"What are you talking about?"

"That was some kind of signal, wasn't it?"

"I don't know what you're talking about."

The therapist rolls off the couch. He's in Jim's face, standing over him, screaming, "Why did you lie to your mother!" He wraps a plump arm around his neck in a headlock and Jim thinks that he can take him, but he just lets the therapist squeeze his neck. He passes out for a while and when he wakes, he is bound to a chair in the attic room.

"Tell me more about Cicely," the therapist says. "Does she arouse you still?"

Who is Cicely? Who was Cicely? Sometimes he thinks that he has dreamed Cicely, that she could not have really been. It will take him years, a lifetime, to realize there will never be another woman who will want him the way Cicely wanted him; no other woman will have Cicely's urgency, the frequency of her urgency.

A twig of a girl. So thin. A dancer's build. Black hair. So straight. Not a hint of a curl. It hangs straight and flat as if ironed, cut straight across just above her eyebrows. Her lips red, lipsticked at a time when natural is in. Brown eyes. She seems not to blink. She looks at all men with those unblinking eyes, smiling, as if each man, the young, the old, the fat, the thin, are all marvelous creatures whom she can appreciate. All are splendid.

But Jim's the real one, the one she really loves. He's the one. He's wanted. She must have him this very minute, at the drive-in, at a park, on a picnic bench, behind the reservoir, on a rooftop, on a hill, at the lake, beneath a bridge. *Tell me you love me, Jim. Come, come, come, look at me when you come!*

I love you! I will!

Cicely, Cicely, Cicely . . .

They break up; they get back together. He hears she's been seen with Bobby G. again; he breaks up again, lies around the house moping, trying not to cry . . .

On the day his family receives notice of Len's death in combat, Jim takes off running up the hill like he's on fire. Runs behind the reservoir, screams down the alleyway, springs over Cicely's fence. Jeeter fixes him with a yellow-eyed glare, shoots across the lawn and rips at his jeans as he bangs on the sliding glass door. When she opens it, he falls into her arms, not taking her down on the couch, which is good because her mother is in the den watching TV. He cries into her and she holds him, crying with him, the two of them shaking and her mother up now, too, figuring it out, her own husband a pilot in the war, and the three of them standing there holding each other and crying, Cicely's mother dabbing at his head, his hair, his shoulders, as if to put out the fire . . .

Through the teen years, driving alone in cars late at night, he screams and beats at the steering wheel . . . Come back, Len, come back, he wishes a million times. A million times a million . . .

After Winning the Nobel Prize, Jim Writes a Letter to His Literary Agent, Toward Whom He May Have Mild Romantic Feelings

For your eyes only:

    There hasn't been anyone to talk to lately. My wife is busy with her own work. And the kids are older now and don't need me so much.

    I came down to this beach town. I found myself brooding over my own life. It frightened me. I want to spend time elsewhere, back on the frontier with my ancestors Tom and Will.

    The people who were my friends have drifted away . . . We don't call each other much anymore. Or write except for forwarded email jokes.

    I'm glad you came down for a day. I kept picturing in my mind that you would. I suppose I was raving. I suppose we won't ever have our affair. I don't have affairs, you know. At least I don't think I do.

But I was happy to walk with you on the beach. I was happy to hold your hand, a slender, fragile hand. So light. Like holding air. I felt my own hand was so hard and calloused and nicked from my years of boxing and deep water fishing.

I was happy when we hooked the marlin. I was glad when we let it go. I'm sorry the boat captain made a pass at you. You were right to Mace him.

For a moment, back on the beach, when you pushed up your sunglasses and swept your hair back from your brow, I almost kissed you. I almost started this affair that cannot happen, that I cannot allow to happen. I do not have affairs. You looked magnificent with your long white shirt open over your black swimsuit. I took a breath and prepared to lunge in. You were right to Mace me.

After you left, I found a gym to work out in. I punched the heavy bag. I sparred with a contender. He beat me senseless. I felt more like myself again.

I'm getting old . . . I need some new tricks . . . a stiffer jab . . .

I've found a beach café with good coffee. I sit beneath a table umbrella and hear snatches of conversation. Everyone is so earnest. They're working out their problems here at the tables. It's okay to be this or that, they say, they've discovered it's okay to behave this way or that. They've learned to accept things about themselves, they've learned how to love themselves unconditionally. They forgive themselves and each other. So what if one is an ax murderer? Sure, there's always room for improvement, but there are reasons for such things, one can't get down about it.

That's good! They say to one another. That's right! Right on!

I treasure my friendships, they say to one another. You have a special place in my life, they say, and that's kind of what it's all about . . . I'm changing . . . I'm growing . . . Growing is good! I'm so happy for you!

They're all growing and changing and forgiving themselves before my eyes, and I am alone. The only image that cheers me is of a golfing quilt I once saw on the Fourth of July in Oregon. Such a great swing! I'd like to buy that little golfer a drink.

In a day or two, no doubt, I will ride the train home and embrace my wife and children and we will resume. We will take it up again, yet again, but for now there is no one to talk to, and only these mad voices inside to listen to . . .

The afternoon wears on and now the conversations dwindle and run dry . . . No one is growing . . . We feel oily and fat . . . We wander off to our rooms . . .

In the night the wind howls at my door. The electricity goes out. I light a candle, take a gingko balboa for clarity, perform a Chi Kung exercise called Old Man Eats Shit. Swooping down and swinging my arms, and as my head comes up dizzily, I leave myself and I am back on the frontier.

In Which Tom Meets Alice

Tom holds the spare horses and watches from a hilltop as the battle rages on. He's got the horses and this would be the perfect chance to escape as the eight braves, led by White Crane, batter at the doors and windows of the cabin and the settlers inside fire through portholes. This attack's gone sour, one brave already killed. The Comanches like surprise attacks, not these pitched battles, and White Crane orders a retreat to the hilltop. Every life is precious. He doesn't want to lose another warrior, but he's lost control of the braves in their blood lust. White Crane looks at his adopted son in despair, shakes his head and rides back in.

Now, Tom thinks, ride away, ride. He can ride through the night and by morning be striking deeper into the settlements, back to safety. But Will's back in the Comanche camp. He can't leave Will. He promised he'd take him home even if Will no longer wants to go home.

The cabin goes up in flames, and Tom tries to close off his ears from the shrieking inside, but out of the flames runs a figure, a woman in a long gingham dress. She screams as the braves encircle her. The back of her dress is lit on fire and White Crane tackles her and rolls in the dirt with her, tumbling over and over to put out the fire, and now a moment later a blazing man, a human torch, flees out of the cabin and the braves shoot him down in a fusillade of bullets as he rushes them.

The braves move in on the woman, but White Crane commands them to stand back. He throws the woman up on a horse, swings in behind her and they ride back up the hill to Tom. He sees her slumped over the horse, though even her slump of despair and shock cannot hide her wholesome Texas country ranch curves, her willowy North Texas supple strength, her raven brown hair; ah yes, she is a beauty, fresh from a burning cabin and he sees her eyes shining at him and imploring. She is about his own age and he says, in English, "Don't worry. I'll get you back home."

She puts her hand to her mouth and bursts into hysterical tears and he realizes he's just said something incredibly stupid. Her home is up in flames. Her people are dead. She has no home.

White Crane spurs his horse and rides off with the woman, and Tom understands. White Crane's affections are sudden and intense; the woman is to be White Crane's wife.

The Word Terrorist

*D*alton, the word terrorist, barges into Jim's office at the college. "I was able to hack into your computer and saw the shit you're writing! My God! It's horrible, but I love it! I'm enjoying every word of it, but unfortunately, I've changed a few of your syllables and you've read them, and I'm going to clear out of here, because in a few minutes, you're going to go stark raving mad!" He howls with glee and cackles as he runs down the hallway.

Jim sits on his hands waiting for the madness to overpower him. But Dalton had not counted on the thin layer of white gas creeping under the door. It's a light gassing President Jammer is giving them this time. It calms Jim, soothes his racing heart.

He dozes. He is at one with Tom on the frontier. A ghost appears to Tom as he wanders alone by the creek near the Comanche camp. Well, not quite alone, for he has come to keep an eye on Alice, the girl taken from the burning cabin. She goes to the creek each day to be alone in the trees, and he wants to make sure she doesn't run off because he knows they will find her and be hard on her. She must wait for the right moment to escape with him and Will. He watches from far enough away not to frighten her, but he wants to be glimpsed. He wants to let her know there is someone watching over her. "Why'd you let them kill me?" the ghost of the old rancher, Alice's father, asks.

"What was I supposed to do?"

"Hell, son, you could have done something. At least expressed your reservations."

"I was just holding the horses."

"Oh, sure, somebody's got to hold the horses." The old man raises a quivering finger, points at Alice, at her buckskinned back as she stares across the prairie, stares south, toward the settlements. "You took her. You bring her back." The old rancher dissolves from view, adding, as he fades, "Stop holding those goddamned horses."

But it's not so easy to keep from holding the horses. Autumn nights in North Texas. Chilly full moon nights. Comanche moons. They ride through the night and fall upon lone cabins like howling ghosts. They've got some repeating guns now, taken from killed settlers. The young braves have lost interest in the bow and arrow, though White Crane tries to teach them, to encourage them. They laugh at him. Daily, he loses more control.

The spirits of the dead, the slaughtered, follow Tom. Holding the horses. Just holding the horses. Meanwhile, Alice and Will await him back in the camp. Will wants to start coming on the raids. Tom can't let him. He can't let him get mixed up in this. He has to take him home before the spirits haunt him as well.

A cabin sits in blackness. They leave the horses with Tom, go on stealthily on foot. He wishes the settlers would wake. Sometimes if they fire from inside the cabin, it's enough to drive the Indians off. But usually the Indians are in on them, battering down the flimsy door before the settlers can react. Then it's the screaming. And Tom's praying the screaming doesn't go on too long.

But there's no screaming from inside this time. What the Indians do not know yet is that they have hit the cabin of Ranger Alvin Johnson, the toughest man north of the Red River, and there are only tough men north of the Red River.

Ranger Alvin lives alone. He likes it that way, a lone man in a lone cabin on the lone prairie. He's been preparing for such a night as this. This is no ordinary front door. No indeed. It's bolstered with iron taken from broken down wagons, burnt out wagons, wagons deserted on the prairie, the bones of their once inhabitants now bleaching in the sun, but that is the cycle of life, where the remnants of dreams are now woven into the doors and window bars and coverings that protect Ranger Alvin's cabin, a veritable fortress.

His ears are well-trained. He has heard these Comanches coming for miles, felt the thud of their horses' hooves sending waves through the darkness, and he is pumped, he is primed. He met an old Chinese man a few years back who taught him mysterious dance-like movements that energize him, send tingles through his arms and legs, so that even at the age of sixty, he is now as spry as a man of thirty-five. And there is something hostile about Ranger Alvin, from many years of riding the plains. He just feels hostile. He's spoiling for a good fight.

When they start battering the door, he lets them. He's curious about just how much pressure that door can withstand. Now they seem to have some sort of big log or something. It thunders against the door, vibrates it a little, but that's all. Now the howling. Oh boy, they're letting out their war whoops, meant to terrify him. *That's* rich. He slides open the artfully designed knee-high metal porthole, and blasts his shotgun into their legs, mows three of them down. *Now* they've got something to howl about.

White Crane gathers one wounded man beneath the arms and drags him back up the hill to where Tom holds the horses. The other Indians join him, dragging the other wounded. They want to go back in. But this time White Crane is insistent. They're cutting their losses, riding back to camp. White Crane mounts his horse. Like a great solemn shadow he sits between them and the cabin. Tom joins him on his own horse; side by side they stare down the others. White Crane's eyes flicker toward him and he realizes something has changed. If White Crane ever doubted his loyalty, his doubts are gone. This is his son. His son! The other braves mutter, but they back down.

The troop rides off, the wounded slumped over their horses. They ride through the darkness when White Crane motions them to stop. He listens. They hear it then, the faint drumbeat of a horse's hooves across the prairie. The whistling whine of a bullet, and one of White Crane's men pitches off his horse.

Ranger Alvin Johnson, a one man army, is taking the fight to them. He wears an iron vest, and his coonskin hat is lined with iron as well. He's got a repeating rifle, three pistols, two bowie knives, and a derringer up his sleeve. If he reaches over his shoulder, he can take hold of a war axe. At a moment's notice, a release catch underneath his horse's belly will produce a sawed off shotgun.

They never see him. They hear the drum of the hooves and the whistle of the bullets and then another man falls.

Finally, it is only White Crane and Tom. They ride for three extra days, leading miles and miles from the camp before following a winding way back through crevices in canyon walls, barely wide enough for one man to ride through at a time.

Trust Issues

In the room above his garage, Jim's therapist tells him to talk about his trust issues.

His friends report to Jim that they have seen Cicely with Bobby G., her old boyfriend. Bobby G., tall, suave, Italian-Mexican looking guy.

What happened? he asks her. Were you with Bobby?

Of course not, Cicely says. I saw him at the Mall and we talked. That was all.

That was all? You saw him at the Mall and talked, and that was all?

We had a Coke at Woolworth's. Okay? We had a Coke.

You had a Coke at Woolworth's? That was all?

Well, okay, and then I gave him a blowjob in his car. Well, she does not admit this, but he can read between the lines. Somewhere before or after this Coke at Woolworth's, she's leaving out the small matter of the blowjob in the car.

Cicely, Cicely, Cicely, your black straight hair, your belly so trim and flat, and your breasts growing now, and I know by now you've grown old like me, but leave a part of you, will you, there forever at the drive-in, tossing sweatily with me, not Bobby G . . .

Were you with him?

With him?

You know what I mean.

She laughs. Of course I wasn't with him. God, how could you think that when I love you?

But there are rumors, whispers, sightings . . .

As he pumps into her at the drive-in, as he moves in and out, she whispers: Look at me, look at me.

In the darkness, he sees her white teeth. A reflected movie light on her pale, tightened brow.

Look at me, she whispers.

He looks.

But don't stop moving.

He sets a steady rhythm, not overly excited. They did this an hour ago. And the night before that. And the night before that, and he's becoming a bit jaded about the whole thing.

I wasn't with him, she whispers. I swear to you, as you move in and out of me, as you move in and out of me, as you come, as we come together, I swear by the joining of our bodies.

The therapist lies on the couch and lets out a long whistling laugh. "This is rich."

"I just didn't know the truth," Jim says. "That was the whole problem. I just didn't know the truth. It was the not knowing the truth that bothered me. It was not knowing who you could trust. If you could trust anybody."

"You didn't know the truth?" The therapist chuckles. "Sure you knew the truth."

"I did?"

"We both know the truth. She was fucking Bobby G.'s lights out."

"You think so?"

"She was fucking half the school. God, Jim, you are such an asshole. Don't you see it? Your first love was a nymphomaniac. Have you kept up with her at all?"

Jim lies on his office floor, in a fury, snarling and trying to break one of the legs off his chair with his bare hands, and he realizes he must have read something that Dr. Dalton, the word terrorist, had written. But what? He tries to be careful, tries to screen out anything Dalton has written. Soon, he fears, he will not be able to read anything at all. The wrong word, the wrong syllable, throws him into a frenzy.

Is it possible his own words could have such an impact? Not arousing fury, perhaps, but love, animated, wondrous thoughts, elevated thoughts, thoughts that will heal, soothe the huddled masses yearning to be free . . . Is that it, then? Is it a battle between Dr. Dalton and him? What if he could counter Dalton, produce a story so full of love that men and women working in spirit-killing corporations might drop their shorts in hallways, make love over copy machines . . . But no, no, he does not mean to advocate promiscuity, only the love-force at work in society, in the work place, in the home. Cicely, Cicely, did he misjudge her? Was she only trying to spread the love-force in her own way? If they had only known how to channel the love-force . . .

For Your Eyes Only

I summon the muses. Come to me, big Ernie, come to me now. A boxing story? Fishing? Hunting? I stalked the fat marlin through the sweet November woods in the Rocky Mountains, a big fish pausing on a broad rock as I took aim . . . I squeeze the trigger careful-like, real careful-like, nice and smooth and slow and careful-like and easy-like.

I attended a parent-teacher conference when one of my kids was seven and the teacher was going on and on about his writing and how it wasn't so hot and all, and she goes on and on and I'm thinking: Geez, I thought his stories were pretty good and all, imaginative, kind of lively, what are we expecting here from a seven-year-old? Chekhov? But she's really raking him, and she's going on about his "P's" and his capital "E's" and it sinks in on me that she's talking about his handwriting. His penmanship.

And it reminds me of one time when I was flying on an airplane with old Ernie and the fellow next to me was wondering what I did and I told him I was a writer and he thought that was great and asked me if it was hard to get all those letters on the little gold trophies. When I said I was a writer, he thought I meant

I was an engraver. Old Ernie thought that was a riot, but after some Pernod at lunch, he got nasty and threw the poor fellow off the plane. Then Fitz stopped by and he and Ernie got loaded and pulled out their penises and compared them, and then J.D. who was sitting across the aisle slipped off to the restroom and we never saw him again.

But I was trying to politely tell the teacher that I didn't give too much of a damn about my kid's penmanship. I wanted to know if the kid could *write*. Did he have the juice?

Later I took him up to the loft and we worked on some stuff—a few b's, a couple of o's. I thought he wrote a mean Z. I mean it was an out of sight Z, and I called his teacher and I screamed: You should see the Z this kid wrote! It's a beautiful Z!

He couldn't write, my mother's ghost is saying on *60 Minutes*. I mean he couldn't handwrite. He drove the poor nuns nuts. They couldn't read a word he wrote. No one had any idea for a long time that he could write.

Mike Wallace gives a small, ironic smile. They didn't think he could write?

That's right. They thought he was slow.

And they said he couldn't write?

They said he couldn't write.

Do you ever wonder what would have happened if he'd believed them?

Oh, he never doubted himself.

Never?

Not for a minute.

Was he . . . arrogant?

It was more like . . .

He knew?

He knew.

He was too arrogant! My younger brother screams, appearing in the studio, an unscheduled appearance. He was an asshole! A real asshole!

Mike Wallace gives his small, ironic smile. So some thought he was a real asshole? Did the nuns think so, too?

Oh my yes, I think they always thought that, my mother says.

I'm back on the plane and the fellow is saying: Engraving? That's a great profession. How do you fit all those letters on those little gold trophies?

The Hound of Death

Ranger Alvin follows the tracks all the way back to camp and he's hidden now somewhere on the edges of the camp in winter, picking the braves off one by one. Go out to gather some wood. The sound of a heavy ax falling against a head, and another one is gone. Sometimes Tom imagines that it's his father, Edmund, come to rescue them.

One morning Ranger Alvin rides through the camp shooting down everyone who comes out of the tipis. White Crane orders Tom to grab Alice and Will and the other children and run into the brush while White Crane rallies the braves for a counterattack.

Ranger Alvin rides into the brush. He's hot on them, breathing heavy, his ax swinging toward the head of a running child when Tom leaps up on the back of his horse and knocks him off. With his heavy armor Ranger Alvin can barely rise, but when he does, he looks into Tom's blue eyes, snarls, "You traitor!"

But Ranger Alvin is surrounded now by braves firing their weapons into him. Most of the bullets and arrows bounce off the armor, though some find their way through. He snarls at them with each new wound. He walks slowly, stiffly, toward one of the horses, leaves the brush as they shower him with arrows and he mounts the horse and he is off, riding across the prairie, but when he gets back to his cabin he falls into a deep depression and during that time he begins to question his ways. Why is it that I have known so much violence, he wonders. Why can't I be at peace with my fellow man? What is it inside of me that has led me to be so out of balance?

And it is said that Ranger Alvin no longer took up arms and was seen gardening, never wearing a stitch of clothing.

A Mysterious Student Drops Off a Story

A knock on his office door makes Jim spring up. It is a young man, Dave, one of his students, handing him a story. "Would you mind if I left this with you to read?" he asks.

Jim stares suspiciously at him. "Did Dr. Dalton send you?"

"Dr. Dalton?"

"Never mind."

He leaves Jim with the manuscript. Jim sits at his desk, groaning. One never wants to be left alone with a student manuscript.

I got drunk a lot back then, the young man wrote.

He groans. Will he have to read a story about a young man getting drunk?

There were two girls . . .

Of course there were two girls. The drunken young man, the two girls . . . We are not off to a promising start here. But at least he is not flying into a rage, so apparently the manuscript wasn't secretly written by Dr. Dalton.

I think they were angels.

Angels?

I got drunk a lot back then. I lived in an efficiency apartment in Austin. I had a bed. I had a kitchen table and a couple of chairs. That was about it. One night the toilet ran over. I didn't know what to do about it. I didn't know anything about toilets, so I just tried to forget about it. I just let it run all night and in the morning I was tramping around the flooded apartment, so I went out for the day and when I came home that night there were the two angels sopping things up. I don't know how they got in. You idiot, they said. Your apartment's flooded. But they were nice about it.

I'd start drinking on one end of Guadalupe Street. I went into a bar on the corner of Guadalupe and Martin Luther King and had a beer and a shot. Then I went up Guadalupe Street to the next bar and I had a beer and a shot. I went up the street like that, stopping at every bar for a beer and a shot. There were seventeen or so bars that I could hit in a few miles. I walked the whole way so it was good exercise and it kept me from putting on weight, and then I'd walk home for miles and sometimes along the way heading home, there the two angels would be—and they'd laugh at me and link arms with me, one on each side of me, and lead me back to my apartment. I could never remember from time to time what their names were, or which one was which exactly. I'd just hear them laugh and there they were. I couldn't even describe them exactly. One of them had bad acne but a great smile. One of them had long blonde hair. It was all very friendly. It wasn't like we were going to have sex or anything.

One night I passed out on the strip of grass outside my apartment complex. There they were, lifting me under the armpits, laughing. You can't sleep here, Dave, they said, and up the stairs we went with their hands supporting me under the armpits. Angels. I read them my poetry. How beautiful, they said, we love it. I don't know what they did during the day. I didn't see them every night. Sometimes I wouldn't see them for a few weeks and I'd think they were gone or wondered if I had imagined them, but then one night they would appear, walking beside me on the sidewalk as I staggered home from the bars. They'd laugh. Are you drunk, Dave?

One night I cried. I guess so, I said. I guess I am drunk. I was twenty-one. I got drunk a lot and wrote poetry. I had a small inheritance from my grandfather. I didn't have to work just then. I went to some classes. I wanted to find some meaning in life. I believed in God, sort of, but I wanted to do things my way. I just wanted an occasional assist from the angels.

At the far end of Guadalupe Street, out where it got kind of wild and weedy, I came to the strip joints.

I fell in love with a stripper named Candy. She was older, twenty-four, and she was gorgeous. I mean, you could see why she was a stripper. You could see the talent there. I guess, technically speaking, she wasn't really a stripper. I mean she didn't really come out with anything much she could strip off. She wore a g-string and pasties over her nipples and that was all except for some kind of gold band around her waist.

I gave her big tips all the time. One night she came home with me after work. We really got it going. We were on the floor for awhile. She danced for me. Then she danced with me inside her. It was incredible.

Somebody banged on the door of my apartment.

"Oh shit," she said. "It's Tiny."

"Who's Tiny?"

"He's going to kill us," she said.

"Oh shit," I said. I knew who he was then. I'd seen him hanging around the strip joint. He was kind of her boyfriend, I guess. A biker. Huge arms, huge gut, about six foot six. Tattoos, leather jacket, chains, knife in the boot, tomahawk on his belt, silver tooth in front.

"I know you're in there!" Tiny roared. "I'm going to kill you!"

"Do you know how to fight?" Candy asked.

"Not all that well," I said.

"We'd better get out of here."

We threw on our clothes, what we could. The door splintered. Tiny busted it down and it fell into the kitchen of the efficiency. He stood there for a moment, looking stunned, as if he hadn't actually expected the door to fall into the room. We screamed and jumped out the back window. We were on the second storey, but we just threw ourselves out and we hit the ground and got up and ran down the alley.

"It's okay," she said, laughing. "We'll go to my place. I'm high as a kite. I can fuck all night when I feel like this."

"That sounds good," I said. "I love you, by the way."

"I love you, too," she said.

I don't think either one of us was entirely sober. She had a little apartment not too far away. As soon as we got inside, we started up again. She was an incredible sight, naked except for that golden band around her waist. Tight hard narrow waist. With twists. These great slopes and twists. We were doing it on her kitchen table. She undulated beneath me. That's the only word I can think of. She undulated. I was on top but it was really more like she was the one in control. I was just following her in some wild wonderful dance.

There was a terrible banging on the door. "I know you're

in there!" Tiny yelled. "I'll kill you!"

We screamed. We threw on our clothes. What we could. I lost a shoe along the way. We jumped out the back window and ran down the alley. I busted my foot some in the fall and I hobbled along but we made pretty good time. We were running hand in hand, laughing. It had started to rain. I told her I loved her again, and told her I wanted to save her.

"I don't want to be saved," she said. "I'm no good."

"You could be. You could change."

She laughed. "Why should I change?"

We slipped into another house. A dumpy old house full of smoke and rotting newspapers and motorcycle parts and grease stains on the floor and roaches scuttling around and a few bikers snoring on the kitchen floor and a tall skinny guy asleep in the fireplace, but it was summer at least so there was no fire going.

"Where are we?" I whispered. I have to admit I was pretty drunk through all this, though all the running had sobered me up some.

She laughed. She had this gleeful, mischievous laugh that drove me wild. A girlish laugh, almost innocent on one level, but sort of wicked, too. "Come in here," she said, and she pushed me into a bedroom and pulled me down on a water bed and I sank way down into her and the bed that smelled of smoke and beer, and each thrust seemed to take us way way down where it seemed like we would not come back up for air.

The bedroom door opened and I turned my head and almost screamed, but Candy covered my mouth with her hand as Tiny came into the room. It was dark, almost black in there except for a little glow from a lava lamp. Tiny made all these grunting and groaning and snorting and farting noises, mumbling and stumbling around in the darkness. "Shit," he said to himself. "Fucking bitch." There was a little sob in his voice as he added, "No feelings. No more. That's it."

I way lying on top of Candy, still inside her, trying to climb out so I could run out of there, but she scissored her strong dancer's legs around my back and held me there. She bit my ear. She was giggling silently. Tiny lay down on his back beside us and started to snore. I felt a little strange about it, but I moved in and out of Candy in a discreet, tender sort of way.

"What do you think?" Dave, his student, asks Jim in his office a few days later.

"Well, it's gritty," he says.

"Do you like it?"

"Well, it was interesting."

"I was reading some of your stuff," Dave says.

"You were?"

"I was kind of rewriting some of your scenes in my mind. Sort of jazzing them up a little. They seemed, I don't know, maybe a little flat."

"Why don't you stick to your own scenes for now? What happened after that? What happened with you and Candy after that? Or does it just end there?"

"Here." He hands Jim another manila envelope, and after he leaves, Jim settles in with a cup of coffee and starts to read. His eyes flicker to a manuscript on his desk. He's been working on a story about a trip the family had taken to Spain the summer before. Maybe the story needs a little jazzing up.

I fell asleep. We both did. Then it was morning. I opened my eyes. I was wedged in the bed between Tiny and Candy. I was right next to him, my face stuck in his hairy armpit. His chest and belly were enormous, his gut jutting up toward the ceiling like some gigantic iceberg. His huge tattooed arm draped around me and snuggled me into him.

Candy was lying on the other side of me, still naked except for the gold band around her waist. She woke when I did and smiled and her hand slid down my belly and started stroking me. I got a hard-on right away.

Some biker poked his head into the bedroom. Same kind of clothes as Tiny's. A tall, really thin guy. So thin he looked like he might be diseased. Scraggly gray beard, wispy long hair. He was the guy from the fireplace.

"Paper's here," he said. Kind of a domestic moment. It was like a ritual for them, you could tell, him and Tiny reading the Sunday paper together.

Candy rolled her head and looked up at him.

"Oh hey, Candy," he said.

"Hey, Sandy," she said. She rose up on an elbow and smiled at him.

"Who's the guy?" he said. But friendly about it. Like I could read the paper, too, if I wanted, after we were done.

She smiled from him to me. Her teeth were white with an attractive little space between the two front teeth. Then she laughed. "I forgot your name. I'm sorry. That's really tacky of me."

"Dave," I said.

"Hey, Dave," Sandy said. "You want coffee?"

"Sure," I said.

He waved a hand as he backed out the door. "Take your time."

Tiny opened his eyes. He blinked like a man waking up out of an accident. My hard-on knocked against Tiny's gargantuan hip. His huge eyes got wider.

He tried to sit up, but Candy dove over me and landed on him, squeezing me out of the way, giggling her mischievous giggle. "Come on, baby," she purred, undoing his belt buckle. "I've been waiting for you to wake up."

She was working on his belt buckle with one hand, while one of his massive hands reached over her and yanked my hair. "Who's the creep?" he said.

"I don't have any idea," she said.

"Get lost, creep," Tiny said. He gave my head a shove. He was starting to make little cooing sounds as her hand snaked inside his trousers. Candy winked at me and signaled with the movement of her head that this would be a good opportunity for me to leave. "Where were you?" Tiny said plaintively, like a little boy.

I grabbed my clothes. What I could. And ran out of the bedroom.

Some of the bikers were starting to stir and roll around on the floor. Sandy turned from the stove in the kitchen. "You ready for coffee?"

I kept going out the front door.

"Nice meeting you, Dave," he called cheerfully.

I hobbled along with no shoes. Then the angels appeared beside me. They had never appeared in broad daylight before. They looked even younger in the light. They seemed a little sad, though. Maybe it was because they were seeing me in the light for the first time, and I must have looked horrible. Oh Dave, they said, what have you been doing? We need to get you home.

It was summer, the nights hot and moist. I told myself to forget about Candy, but the days went by and I couldn't stop thinking of that gold band around her waist. I stayed away from the topless bar for two weeks, but couldn't stand it. I slipped back in there one night and sat in the darkness with a beer and watched her dance on the stage. She danced like she was on fire inside. She massaged her breasts, ran her fingertips along the insides of her thighs. She really loved dancing, you could tell. She was in some place all her own, like she was listening to some other voice, some other spirit, in her own time, her own world. She never really looked my way, or if she did her eyes just swept over me like I was just another one of the inhabitants of the darkness.

I came back in again the next night, but this time I sensed that she knew I was there. I followed her around the bar with my eyes, from when she was on stage to when she was serving drinks. But she didn't come to my table. I had a sense she'd sent another barmaid my way on purpose. But I kept coming back, and two nights later, without warning, she sat down at my table. She was wearing a black halter top. She looked almost sexier than when she was bare. Her nipples pressed against the cloth. I could hardly say hello. My voice cracked and stuck. "I missed you," I heard myself saying.

"Do I know you?" she said. She looked hard at me, she blinked. She smiled that beautiful smile with the little space between her front teeth. "Oh yeah. You. That was fun."

"I love you." My voice came out in a dry, crazy whisper. She gave me a serious look. "Don't get mixed up with

me. It's not worth it." Then she laughed again, that wicked laugh, and she gave my nuts a squeeze under the table, and then she was up, doing a shuffling dance away from me, wiggling her ass in a taunting sort of way.

I sat there and got drunk. Drunker than usual. The next thing I knew somebody was beating me up in the parking lot outside the club. There's a curious, heavy, going down feeling when you're drunk, real drunk, going down down down, like you're watching yourself go down but you can't do anything about it, and then I hit the pavement. I felt a few kicks in my side, but they didn't hurt too much. The guy didn't seem all that much into it. I covered up and after a while he got bored and wandered away.

I walked home all bloody. The angels found me along the way. They sighed and clucked over me and led me back to my apartment and cleaned me up and bandaged me. I told them about Candy.

Go away somewhere, the angel with the bad acne and the beautiful smile said. Go away until you're over her.

I decided they were right. I took a train down to Mexico. Way down to the interior. For a while, nine months or so, things went along great. I lived in an old colonial town with cobblestone streets. I wrote stories. I still drank, but I didn't get so drunk most of the time. I met another angel. I couldn't ever remember her name. She'd show up when I was walking home from the bars. She was some sort of model back in the States, she said, though she wasn't one of those super thin models. She was fairly thin, but not super thin. She felt wonderful to hold. But that's all that ever happened. She'd show up late at night and we'd smooch in a doorway on a cobblestone street. I'd hold her for a while and we'd smooch and then she'd be on her way and I wouldn't see her for another week or so. Usually she showed up by just suddenly holding my hand. I mean, I wouldn't even see her coming, then all of a sudden she'd be holding my hand and smiling. She didn't say much, she wasn't really much of a conversationalist. If she hadn't always been slipping away and disappearing, I would have fallen in love with her. I'd walk around town all day during the daylight, but I could never find her.

I thought I was over Candy. I took a train back to the border, but I did something stupid there. Instead of crossing the border, I spent the day drinking in Nuevo Laredo, and at night, I found myself at the whore houses. I don't know why. I didn't even want a whore. I was just there. It was pretty dismal. I went into a room with a plump Mexican woman. She lifted up a rubber bag and said we should clean up a little first. She had a plump, smooth belly but sad looking lopsided little breasts. I got really depressed and before we did anything, I said I needed to go. She was pissed at me. She followed me to the door and squirted something from the rubber bag onto the back of my shirt.

Out on the street I weaved between bars. It looked like sort of an old western town out of the movies.

A woman shouted at me from a dark doorway. "Two dollar, sucky fucky, two dollar, sucky fucky!"

Maybe I wasn't entirely sober, but I went up to her and I saw that she was old and toothless and she said, "You want sucky fucky?"

"No," I said. "That's the last thing I want. I'm taking you out of here."

I had some crazy notion that I needed to get this poor old woman out of this hellhole. It suddenly burned in me, this sort of desire that I needed to free her from this place, that no woman, no human being on earth, should inhabit such a hellhole.

I took her by the arm and started dragging her down the street and she started screaming. She screamed bloody murder like I was crazy or something.

I heard shouts and footsteps coming my way and I kept dragging her as she kept screaming and my thought was she would be happy once I got her out of there, she would see that it was better in the outside world. The shouts grew louder and I had a sense of being surrounded, a flashlight blinded me, and then something slammed into the back of my head and I went down.

When I awoke it was morning, the sun just coming up, and I was lying on my side in the desert, my hands tied behind my back. As I came to and sat up, I heard a man screaming. He was surrounded by several other men. There were a couple of pickup trucks in the desert with us. The men pushed him down on a boulder and hacked him with machetes while he screamed horribly.

I realized I was sitting next to another man, tied up like me. Except he wasn't being still. He was working his hands behind his back, trying to free himself from the ropes. I started trying that myself. "Take your fingers," he said, "and work on my ropes." He pressed his back against mine, and I started working on his ropes.

The man was still being hacked to death. It was hideous the way he was screaming. I had a splitting headache and was having a hard time processing all this.

"I'm an undercover cop," the man behind me said in accented English. "I have a gun in my boot."

The man was finally still, dead on the boulder, and the men came for us now, six of them, some carrying machetes, some carrying pistols and rifles. They took me first, lifting me up and dragging me toward the boulder, but the dead man was still on it, hacked up, and they rolled him off it and started to push me down. One of the men raised a machete over my head and I shut my eyes.

I heard the first shot and I opened my eyes and saw the guy with the machete dropping with blood spurting out of his head. The undercover agent was up and running right at the men, firing as the men tried to fire back at him. I got off the boulder and charged a man who was aiming a gun at the agent. I threw myself into him and knocked him off balance. He pitched to the side and the agent was a foot away from him now and he fired twice into his chest. They were all down now and he went around and fired a few more shots here and there into their bodies.

The agent went around taking their wallets out of their pockets, taking the cash and throwing the wallets back on their dead bodies. The agent untied my hands. I recognized one of the wallets as mine and reclaimed it. The agent handed me a big bunch of cash, some in dollars, some in pesos.

"I don't want it," I said.

"Take it," he said. "It'll just end up with a crook."

I didn't really want to, but he kept poking the bundle at me so I slipped the money into my own wallet. It was stuffed. I had thousands of dollars.

We saw a cloud of sand and dust, kicked up by another pickup truck coming our way. "Oh shit," the agent said. "We'd better get out of here."

We got in one of the pickups. The keys were in there. We

rolled out of there. The agent handed me a gun. "If they get too close, fire a few shots out the window."

They got a little too close and I fired a few shots out the window and the pickup truck slowed and let us roll on through the desert. By late morning, we were back in Nuevo Laredo and the agent dropped me off with the border crossing in sight.

"Don't you need me to be a witness or anything?" I asked.

He shook my hand. "I think it's best if you just go."

That whole episode must have stirred something up inside of me because that night, back in Austin, I bought a cheap used beater of an old Mustang for six hundred dollars in cash and found myself going into the bar where Candy worked. My idea was that I would drive away with her in the car, rescue her from the bar where she was working. It had been nine months, though, and I wondered if she still worked there.

I sat in the cool darkness. It occurred to me that I was home. I was in my element. I love the cool darkness of a bar, the air conditioner blowing. That's it. That's my life. There was a moment of peace there where I knew I would be okay, where I knew I didn't need Candy. All I needed was a place like this, a cool dark place with the air conditioning pumping, maybe some music playing, some dancers on stage wasn't bad, but I didn't really need them.

But then Candy came out on the stage and suddenly I was trembling all over. Something was wrong. She was thinner. Still beautiful. Maybe even more beautiful. But thinner, sleeker, her ribs showing. She looked like a creature out of the jungle. I just stared at her. You know that expression, your heart goes into your throat. I actually felt like that. I finally knew what that expression meant. I just stared, my heart in my throat. There was something else wrong. She wasn't wearing the gold band around her waist. I was sure someone had stolen it from her. Someone had treated her cruelly and taken her gold band.

I stared at her all through her set. Dancers feel it when you're watching. When you're watching quietly and appreciatively and not hooting and hollering and whistling like a fool. She stared back at me, finding me in the darkness and she tantalized her nipples with her fingertips. One pasty had fallen off, which is illegal. There seemed something wrong with her, something disoriented or frightened, as if she'd left the regular world, as regular as her world had ever been.

After her set, she came straight to my table and sat down. "Hey good-looking," she said. "What do you look so sad about?"

My voice was stuck. After a few swallows, I said, "You used to wear a gold band around your waist."

She stared at me. "Do I know you?"

"You don't remember me?"

"Are you some kind of weirdo?"

"No. I mean, I don't know. You don't have to worry about me or anything. I'm harmless."

"I doubt that," she said. "Stick around. I've got to wait tables and dance again."

The next time she danced just for me. You can tell that sort of thing. She undulated.

After her dance, she sat back down. "What am I supposed to remember? I mean, did we fuck?" She smiled at me. "Isn't that weird? Are you bullshitting me?"

"Tiny kept breaking down the door. We ended up in bed with him."

She stared at me. "Son of a bitch," she said. "I remember you now."

"How's Tiny?"

Her eyes went hollow, and her cheeks sucked in. "He's dead." She gripped my hand and her face suddenly turned fearful. I mean really scared. "Look," she said. "There's something you don't understand. There's some bad shit going on."

"I can take you out of it."

"What are you talking about?"

"Come with me to Mexico. I have money. I have a car waiting outside."

She swept her long blonde hair back. She was gorgeous. "Are you sure you can handle me?"

"Let's go."

She looked around. "I'm probably being watched right now. I'm going to go to the back and get dressed. Wait for me outside in the back parking lot. Have your car ready. I mean it, it's bad shit. They'll kill us both if they think I'm trying to get away."

"I'll have the engine running."

"Don't be fucking obvious about it. Have another beer before you get up."

She gave my nuts a quick rub under the table. She disappeared into the back of the bar and I drank another beer and made some nonchalant breathing noises. I clapped at the other dancers as if I were just another fan, and then I slipped out the door.

I pulled my old Mustang into the back parking lot and sat with the engine running. It was an old battered car already, and I feared it would get worse. I wasn't a very good driver and I tended to bump into things, though I was very careful.

I wanted to leave it somewhere as soon as possible.

I watched the back door of the bar. A tall curly-haired guy came out. He walked right up to my car and opened the door and sat down in the passenger seat. "Look, this is the deal," he said, looking straight ahead and not at me, his hands on his knees. "Candy doesn't need this."

"Who are you?" I asked.

"I'm her doctor," he said.

"Her doctor?"

"She's a patient of mine from the mental hospital."

I remembered there was a mental hospital just down from the bar. I had walked past it many times. Sometimes I had longed to climb over the fence and take refuge below the oak trees.

"She's delusional," he said. "I want to check her back into the hospital."

The door opened. It was Candy. She was wearing a black halter top and blue jean cut-offs. Her face was fearful but she looked incredible. "Get out, Curtis," she said.

The curly-haired man started crying. "I love you," he said. But he got out.

The moment he did, Candy slid in and said, "Drive!"

We drove off for the border. We didn't talk for half an hour. She sat slumped against the door smoking cigarettes. "Who did he say he was?" she asked finally.

"He said he was your doctor from the mental hospital."

"This is so much shit," she said. "He's insane. Maybe he was a doctor at one time, but now he's just crazy."

"You're not from . . . "

"Are we going to bring up a bunch of shit?" she said. "Or are we going to have a good time."

*We stopped at an all-night diner and she began to feel
cheerful again. She wolfed down a huge breakfast. She smiled
at me. "I think I was a little hypoglycemic," she said. "Now
I'm feeling good. I'm feeling real good." She winked at me.
"Is your back seat clean?"*

"It's clean."

*We found a deserted road and made love in the back seat.
She didn't make a lot of noise but she kept breathing in my
ear the whole time, this wonderful little song-like breathing.
We both fell asleep so it was morning by the time we hit Laredo. I left the car at a long term parking on the American
side. Our train didn't leave until evening so we spent the day
shopping for some clothes for Candy, first in Laredo and then
on the Mexican side, in Nuevo Laredo. She was cheerful the
whole time, sort of skipping on the sidewalks, in the stores
whirling around and prancing for me as she tried things on,
then giving me these sort of shy looks as if maybe I'd think
she looked funny in something.*

*We bought the tickets and sat in the train station in Nuevo
Laredo. I saw a man standing a little ways off across the station talking to two rough-looking men and then he broke off
from the men and stared at me in astonishment. I realized he
was the undercover agent who had saved my life. I started to
get up, but he warned me away with a look and turned back
to the two men and started walking with them. He glanced
back at me with a look of sheer disbelief. What in the hell was
I doing back in Mexico? I gave him a little shrug of my head
and tried to encompass Candy's presence with the look, as
if that might say it all. Men had done crazier things for love.*

*We stood between the train cars and screamed into the
blackness of the night. "I'm in fucking Mexico!" Candy*

screamed in delight, hugging me. "I've never been in fucking Mexico before! I love you, Mexico!"

"Mexico loves you!" I screamed back ecstatically.

We made love in our compartment to the bucking and swaying of the train and maybe it had something to do with the loud clacking of the train wheels, but she really cut loose. Her fingernails clawed at my back and she belted out wild moans and screamed, "Fuck me! Fuck me! Fuck me for Mexico!" I felt like the luckiest man alive.

Later we went to the club car, but we both only had coffee. It was like we were getting serious. "Wow," she said as we crossed the desert in the night, seeing little campfires off in the distance. "Look," she said, "I'm not crazy if that's what you're wondering. I was a little messed up at one point and I did forty days and they let me out. They said I was fine. Curtis was one of my doctors back then. He was the crazy one. He had a thing about me. I don't even think he works there anymore."

"What kind of trouble are you in?"

She talked low so that the other people in the club car wouldn't hear, but nobody was paying any attention to what we were saying. They were just staring at her because she was so beautiful.

"They killed Tiny," she whispered.

"Who did?"

"The rug dealers," I thought she said. It was hard to hear over the train wheels and the other conversations.

"Why would rug dealers kill Tiny?" I asked.

She looked at me like I was an idiot. "The drug dealers," she said. "Tiny fucked them over. You don't fuck over the drug dealers."

From my own incident the day before, I knew there were dangerous people in the world. "I guess not."

"They shot Tiny dead. They killed Sandy, too." Tears welled up in her eyes. "Sandy was nice."

"Yes, he was," I said. "I'm sorry."

"It wasn't fair. He never messed with anybody. He was in Vietnam. He had a bad leg."

"I'm sorry about Sandy. Tiny, too, though I think he had some problems."

"Tiny was a bastard," she said. "He had no reason to be mean. He just was."

"Why are they after you?"

"I saw it. I saw them kill Tiny and Sandy. I hid in the bathroom but I saw it through a crack in the door. I know who they are."

"Do they know?"

"They suspect, I think. I called the police. Anonymous. I don't want to be involved in this shit. They'll kill me. But I don't like what they did to Sandy. He sat down when they shot him. He sat down on a kitchen chair and he said, 'Aw, don't do that,' like he was more tired than hurt. Then he fell over. Then they started for Tiny. 'Hey, hey don't, man!' he screamed and he backed up onto the bed. 'Hey!' he screamed, 'hey don't!' like they would give a shit, and then they blew off his head with a shotgun."

Candy was crying. "He used to hit me," she said. "But he loved me. He was backing away as far from the bathroom as he could so they wouldn't see me."

I handed her a napkin and she dabbed at her eyes while I kissed the backs of her hands. "Sandy was nice. I used to think me and Sandy might . . . But Sandy wasn't like that.

I don't think he liked girls that way. He wasn't gay, but he wasn't interested that way. He was like an old man in some ways. It was like he'd gotten everything out of his system a long time ago. He just liked working on his bike and doing art. He did these paintings. They were beautiful. Skies and flowers and cactus and skulls and deserts. They were awesome . . . I told him, Sandy, you've got to take these to a gallery. Aw, he said, they ain't so good. Sandy, I said, if you won't take these to a gallery, I will. I'll fuck somebody to get these in a show if I have to.

"They smashed them up. The bastards smashed up all the paintings before they killed Sandy. 'Now, aw, don't do that,' Sandy said every time they smashed one. It was terrible. It was like he was watching something that he loved die. 'We'll give you your money back,' Tiny told them. 'We'll give you more.' He begged them. They just laughed."

Candy and I took the train all the way to Mexico City. We stayed in the Zona Rosa in a beautiful hotel. We had an old fashioned elegant room with a chandelier. We took long baths together in a claw-footed tub. We ordered food in. One day we were walking around the Zona Rosa and she got very mischievous. She told me to wait outside a store and she went in. "What did you buy?" I asked when she came out. She giggled. This delightful giggle. She looked like a high school cheerleader when she giggled like that. I even noticed the freckles on her cheeks for the first time. I asked her to marry me. I felt incredibly happy all of a sudden, but incredibly sad, too. I wanted to take away all the crazy years. I wanted to be back in high school with her, just starting out, nothing gone wrong in our lives, no damage done.

I kept asking her what she'd bought, and she kept giggling and acting mysterious, but she liked being asked, liked that I was buying into the game.

That night she went into the bathroom and when she came out she was naked except for the gold band that she'd bought in the store. There it was. Around her beautiful waist with its wonderful twists and slopes. "Ta duh," she said, raising her arms like a prize winner. Giggling, she spun around. She danced around the room for me, flying and whirling, up on the bed, on chairs, on a dresser, coming over to rub my nuts, swooping on. She spun, she twirled, she pirouetted. She gave it everything she had until she fell on the floor out of breath, curled on her side, panting and sweating. She rested for half a minute and then she rolled on her back and stuck her pelvis up in the air. She undulated. God, I'd go back there in a minute. If I could go back to one minute in my life, that would be it, Candy twirling around that room in Mexico City.

I was in love. One day we took a subway out to Chapultepec Park and toured around Maximilian's Palace and all that. We read about Maximilian and Carlotta, their disasters in Mexico and the execution. It was big news to Candy. She was amazed. She was blown away by them, by what happened. She had tears running down her face.

When we went back to the hotel and rode up in the elevator I knew something was wrong. She sat down on one of the queen beds. "They're here," she said.

It chilled me the way she said that. "Who is here?"

"The killers," she said. "I saw them in the park, near the swans."

There was a sudden knock on the door and I almost screamed. I looked out with the chain still locked, but it was only the maid with some towels.

Candy was sitting on the edge of the bed. She clutched herself and shook like she had a fever.

"I want to get out of here," she said. "I want to go to the ocean."

I held her. "Okay," I said. "Sure. We'll go to the ocean."

She rolled over and lay on her side and I just held her like that, lying against her. In the morning, we took a bus to the Pacific Ocean and checked into a little white hotel. One day we went out on the beach, around a bend in the sand, away from the town and any people, and she took off all her clothes and started swimming out. I called out to her. She kept swimming out. Suddenly I knew what she was up to, and I didn't even take off my clothes, I just kicked off my sandals and went after her.

I wasn't in too good of shape from all the drinking the last couple of years, but I was a good swimmer. I'd been on my high school swim team. I caught up with her. She fought me, scratching and clawing at my face. Then she wrapped those strong dancer's legs around my waist and brought me down with her. We were sinking together. I didn't fight any more. I thought, okay, then, if that's what she wants, I'll end it now, with her. Then her legs let me go, released me. I couldn't help myself. I broke for the surface. I hated myself for that, but I couldn't help it. My mind was saying one thing, but my whole body was screaming: Breathe! Breathe! My head burst through the water and I gasped for air.

I propelled myself downward, groping through the water for her, but it was murky and my eyes filled up with salt water. I couldn't see a thing. I came up for air. I called her name over and over, and I wanted to die myself. I would swim out and out until I went under for good.

I heard a laugh and looked toward shore and she was in the breakers, rolling herself over and over toward the beach.

I followed her in and when she got to shore, she started walking toward the hotel, not bothering to put on her clothes. I picked up her clothes from the sand and followed her, calling, "Candy! Candy, put on your clothes!"

I sounded like an old man. I sounded like the responsible one. It was strange to find myself in that position.

I caught up with her, tried to wrap a towel around her, but she shook it off. She hardly slowed down. "It's all bullshit," she said. "It's all bullshit."

"Candy," I said, "you've got to put your clothes on."

She stopped for just a moment, and her eyes looked through me, dull and flat, as if she felt nothing for me. "You can't save me," she said.

Then she walked on, and as we came around the bend, there were other people on the beach, regular people out swimming or lounging on towels. Mexico is a curious sort of country. You can get away with a lot, be forgiven for a lot, but there are things you can't get away with and one thing you can't get away with is walking through a public area naked, so when Candy kept going and went into the hotel and through the lobby and up the stairs, I knew there'd soon be a knock on our door so I was already packing when the knock came.

The hotel clerk and the policeman were actually quite nice about it. From the doorway, they could see Candy sitting on the bed, shaking. The moment we'd hit the hotel room, she became more modest and now she did have a towel wrapped around her. She gave them a friendly, timid little wave and there was something fragile and frightened about her, so the hotel clerk, with the policeman standing behind him, his hand resting on the top of his nightstick, just said that we would have to leave.

We took a bus to the next town over and from there we were able to get on a train. It wasn't the same sort of ride back. We just sat in the Pullman, staring out the window. We hardly talked. We didn't even drink.

In Laredo, we picked up my car and drove back to Austin, mostly in silence, stopping at a diner to get a bite to eat.

When we got into Austin, she said, "I need to go back."

I knew what she meant. I drove her to the mental hospital and we passed through the wide gates and drove up a winding hill beneath huge oak trees that shaded the whole road, that seemed to shade everything, as if one could walk through the hottest day in peace and comfort and quiet. She knew the whole procedure. She got checked in at an old red brick building with an antiseptic smell. She was nice and quiet and polite with the woman at the desk and with the white-suited attendants who came for her. They all seemed to know her and to like her. Before they took her off to the ward, she kissed me softly on the lips. Then she stepped back and looked at me calmly and said, "I don't want to see you again."

"I love you," I said.

"Then stay away. You're no good for me."

I don't know why exactly, some kind of hurt or something, but I went back to the club that night.

I guess I shouldn't have been too surprised. There was Tiny hanging out in the pool room. There was Sandy. Both of them. Alive.

A few days after Jim reads his story, Dave comes into his office.

"What did you think?"

"Not bad," Jim says. "Interesting." He looks out the window. Picks up his manuscript about the family summer trip to Spain, fiddles with the edges of the manuscript. "Hey," he says, "would you mind looking at this? Maybe help me jazz it up a little?"

Escape

Tom knows he must save Alice. She complies with White Crane, but does not give White Crane any love or enthusiasm. White Crane is sad. He wants her love. He wants a happy family. He does not know that Tom loves Alice and that it makes Tom furious to see her with him.

One night, in the dead of winter, just as White Crane is settling down with Alice for the night, Tom wallops him in the back of the head with the blunt side of a tomahawk. White Crane keels over on the bearskin blankets. Will is still asleep, so before he can protest or raise an alarm, Tom and Alice tie his hands and feet and gag his mouth.

They carry the squirming little bobcat out to the horses and they set out in a blizzard.

A white-out. Riding through the dread winter with the beautiful young woman and the wild beast of a tied brother.

The great whirling whiteness. He's suddenly horrified to realize that Will isn't on his horse any more. His brother. The person he loves more than anyone or anything in the world, even Alice, is lost in the white whirling madness. He screams Will's name into the white vastness. Sees faintly a figure through falling sheets of snow. He rides back and lifts the nearly frozen body from the snow. He leads them into a grove of trees. They take shelter. He digs a snow cave.

White Crane wakes with a howl of grief. He does not think of revenge, only of regaining his wife and children. They have gone mad. They must come back to their senses. He must save them. He gathers a band of warriors and sets off in pursuit. The other warriors ride without much enthusiasm. They think White Crane might be better off without this lot. They worry he's starting to lose it.

⁕

Edmund, father of Tom and Will, drives his wagon toward Fort Belknap. No hope really. It's just what you do when you hear captives have been brought in.

Tom and Will, after straggling half-frozen into the fort, wait with the other children in a makeshift holding cell in one of the barracks. Alice has already been claimed by an uncle. There is a guard at the cell because the children often run off to rejoin the Comanches. They think they are in the clutches of the enemy.

Will is furious with Tom for bringing them here. He misses the camp, misses White Crane. He cries every night. They hardly recognize themselves with their baths, their haircuts, their white man's clothes.

Tom misses Alice. She was one of the lucky ones. She had an uncle who loved her, who wanted her back. He can hardly picture his real parents now, after six years. When he was first taken, he had thought of nothing but them. He had hated the Comanches. But that began to change as they treated him kindly, as one of their own. Are they his real people now? He has fought for so long to keep the memory of his old life, but he no longer knows if he has an old life to return to.

He struggles to summon his father up. A bearded laughing man, hoisting him and tossing him up in his bunk bed. A moment of giddy flight before landing in the soft warmth of blankets and pillows. The fisherman's toss, his father had called it. Ready for the fisherman's toss, Tommy old lad?

A winter's day, a week before Christmas, and Edmund drives the wagon through the snow to Fort Belknap to take a look at the boys who certainly won't be his boys . . .

No use getting the hopes up. No joy in life now. Memories. A broken heart. Everything you ever dreamed of up in smoke . . . futility . . . futility . . . endure . . .

He pauses beside a chilly creek. An idea comes over him. A strong and alluring desire to hang it all up. To go sit beside the creek and pull his gun and end it, fall on his side and let the snow cover him up. What is it that keeps a man going?

He drives on. Past hope. But full of longing which springs up dangerous as a snake as he drives the wagon through the gates of Fort Belknap.

Tom's remembering the soaring moment of flight as his father tossed him over the top railing of the bunk bed . . . Ready for the fisherman's toss, Tommy old lad?

Sullivan, he whispers to himself. I'm Tom Sullivan. You're Will Sullivan, he says to his younger brother. You're Will Sullivan. Shut up, Will says in the Comanche tongue. Whatever words Tom is speaking are horrible words, horrible English words, he wants nothing to do with them.

Why has Tom brought him here? He wants to go home. Back to his father. Back to White Crane. There's nothing, nothing in Will's memory of the old home, not even an image . . .

Mother singing? Mother reading?

Shut up! Will says fiercely.

But his lips move as if something is trying to dent the block.

I can't, he says to Tom in Comanche, nothing comes back.

So Tom loans Will his own memory. Makes it Will who is being given the fisherman's toss, Will landing amidst soft blankets and pillows.

Will shuts his eyes. They sit side by side against the adobe wall, closing out everyone, the soldiers, the other returned children.

Will he even know his own father if he comes? What if he does not know his father and his father does not know him? What if his father does not want him back?

Edmund has not changed so much physically in the last six years. There's more gray in his beard now. The crow's feet have deepened around his eyes. But the biggest change is a more subtle one. There is no more laughter in his face. It is as if someone has turned a light off.

No more, Edmund thinks, as he ties up the horse and wagon to the hitching post and walks with the sergeant toward the barracks. No more. This is the last time. He won't go through this again. The boys must be dead by now. They'll never come back. It's over. That part of his life is over. Leave it at that.

He has searched and searched. Ridden the badlands with the Rangers. Been away so much he hardly knows Rebecca any more or his little girl, Ellie. He has seen things that have changed him. Come across burned out cabins, mutilated bodies. Seen also the terrible things the Rangers have done as they wiped out camps of the Comanches, the slaughter of women and children, even friendly ones. He has witnessed horror, has been powerless to stop it. A merciless, pitiless war.

And even if you do get your children back, what then? Some friends did. Brought back a seventeen-year-old, Tom's age. He slipped off in the night, went back to the Indians. They can't come home. They've turned wild, their hearts still out on the prairie. Kinder to let them be.

The settlers come and go through the holding barracks, looking over the children.

A stocky bearded man enters the barracks. But it is not his father. His father's face was sunshine and laughter. This man's face is tired and gloomy and fearful.

The man looks at Will and him as they sit against the wall, crouches down to look at their faces. He licks his dry lips. Mumbles to the escorting sergeant who stands over them. Mumbles as if soup is dripping out of the corners of his mouth and gathering in his beard. His shoulders sag. His eyes fall away from the boys.

He rises. Walks out in the snowy quadrangle of the fort. The snow has stopped falling. Now it is a bright, piercing winter day.

Edmund lowers his shoulders, wags his neck like a tired old bull. He loosens the bandana around his throat. He breathes with difficulty, chest tight. A look at the sky. His lips tremble. He remembers the cautions: Do not tell them your name; they may claim to be yours, do not use their names, they may think they are those boys. You may not recognize them, they may not recognize you. They won't be as you remembered them. The child you loved will be no more. They may feel nothing for you. They may hate you. They may blame you for being taken. They may hate you for being returned. They may want nothing of your clothes, your smell, your food, your religion. Your whole way of being in the world may revolt them. They may not want to come back; you may not want them back. You may wish that they were dead so you can remember them the way they were.

The sergeant comes out of the holding cell and his hand falls on Edmund's back. "I'm sorry, mister," the sergeant says.

Edmund's voice chokes up. "I've ridden . . . I've looked . . . I've prayed . . . "

The sergeant spits. "The damn Comanches."

"We've killed their children, too. I've seen it . . . I've . . . I've got blood on my own hands."

The sergeant stiffens. "Now, sir."

"We do. We kill them, too. Women and children . . . "

"Get a hold of yourself, sir."

He turns, grips the sergeant's shoulders with his strong hands. "How many did we kill? How many parents did we leave crying?"

"We're talking about the goddamn Comanches, sir." The sergeant touches the butt of his holstered pistol. He spits, and the toe of his boot mixes the great brown loogey into the sand. "I wouldn't want none of those boys back. They've gone over. They ain't right."

Edmund's hands twitch. He could go for the sergeant's windpipe. Rip it out. It wouldn't take much . . .

"Those are my boys," he whispers. His throat is closing off.

"No, sir," the sergeant says. "You're imagining things. I've seen this happen many times. There's only so much misery a man can take. The mind just snaps." He drapes a heavy arm around Edmund's shoulders, tries to lead him away. "It's a damn shame. They're worthless now. Better to shoot them and be done with it." His eyes narrow and his voice turns to a raspy whisper. "I could do that for you. Take them out tonight on detail, put a bullet in them."

Edmund rolls his shoulders, weaves, and delivers a punch to the sergeant's solar plexus. The sergeant has never been punched by an ex-professional boxer before. It's a stunning experience.

All the breath goes out of him. He doubles up. Edmund leaves him gut-punched and dry puking in the snowy quadrangle.

He comes back through the door, into the dimness and squalid scent of the air. Stares at the boys from just inside the doorway. Can't speak. Stretches a shaking hand out for the boys.

Tom's heart lurches.

The man's voice quavers. "Tom? Will? Boys?"

With a keening wail, Tom hurls himself at his father. Edmund collapses with him to the ground. They clench together, sobbing, rolling about on the dirt floor in a death grip and Edmund thinks through the madness of his emotions: how strong he is, how strong my son has become.

It's minutes, the both of them crying, before he can free himself and go to Will, who sits stone-faced, arms wrapped around his knees. He stares ahead, jaw tightened.

Edmund squats in front of him. Then kneels down before the boy as if begging forgiveness. "Will?"

A boy across the room stands up and shouts, "I'm Will! I'm Will, Daddy, take me home!" He runs to Edmund, throws himself around Edmund's legs.

"I'm Will, Daddy!" the boy shrieks, "Take me home! Take me home!"

The sergeant staggers in, drags the shrieking child from Edmund, pulls him into a corner and beats at him.

Edmund grabs him in a headlock, drags him off the boy.

"Kill them!" the sergeant screams. "Kill them all!"

The captain comes in with two soldiers. They restrain the sergeant, drag him away kicking and screaming.

The captain stands over Edmund. "You're sure?" he says. "Don't rush."

Edmund reaches out to touch Will's cheek. He traces the

line of his jaw with his fingertip. Will snaps his teeth, getting a
piece of the finger.

Edmund cries out and flinches away. He gives a mad laugh
of joy. "It's Will!" he shouts deliriously. "It's my Will!"

He scoops Will up, does a kind of wild dance with him
across the cell as Will kicks and flails at him. The other strange
young boy lies in the corner crying, "Take me home, Daddy,
take me home!"

And in the coming months, Edmund almost wishes at times
that he had taken that poor boy home instead of Will. The only
reason Will does not run away is because of Tom. He has brought
home a wild child, a creature from another world. The boy will
not speak except through Tom. He speaks Comanche to Tom,
who translates for him, though Tom often chooses not to translate accurately.

They're at the dinner table, an evening in spring. They have
prayed, blessed the food.

Will won't touch his dinner.

"Is there something wrong with the meat?" Rebecca asks.

Tom starts to translate, and Will says, "I know what she said.
Tell her I want raw meat."

"I don't want to tell her that."

"Tell her I want to eat the bloody liver of a buffalo."

"You tell her."

"I don't speak her language."

"You just don't want to."

"Why should I? I'm Comanche."

"You're not Comanche. You're white like me."

"Tell her I want raw meat."

Rebecca looks at Tom. "What does he say is wrong?"

"I think he wants his meat a little more rare."

"It is rare."

"I mean you might try . . . not cooking it."

Edmund laughs. Tries to make the best of it. Like always. "Kind of a trail rider's steak?" He winks at Tom, at Will. His chuckles fade under Rebecca's stern gaze.

"Tell your brother," she says slowly, "that we eat our meat cooked in this house. We are not savages."

"She said . . . "

"I know what she said." Will stares at her. He lifts a hunk of meat in his hands and lifts it to his mouth.

"We use a knife and fork in this home," she says. "We showed you. Now do it."

He snarls and throws the steak across the table. It strikes her in the nose, leaves a trail of grease across her cheek and drops into her lap. Edmund stares and holds his breath.

She sits unmoving, grease on the side of her nose. She picks the steak up from her lap and lets it fly at his face.

The steak bounces off his head and drops to the floor. He stares at her, startled. Ellie covers her mouth and giggles. Rebecca dips her hands in her mashed potatoes and flings a handful in Will's face.

Will goes for his carrots. Then they're all in the thick of it, food flying everywhere, as Ellie cries giddily, "This is fun! We've never done this before! We're having fun!"

For Your Eyes Only

$\mathcal{J}$ jogged around a lake this morning. A mountain lion chased me. I thwarted it with a quick twirling motion followed by a sidekick. But that won't put it off for long. It will be after me again tomorrow. The mountain lion situation is bad here. They're dragging down joggers by the dozens. You can hardly water your lawn without one springing over the hedges at you.

But I don't want to bore you with tales of suburbia. You and I are different, we will roam the cobblestone streets of southern Spain, Grenada, with plenty of dough from our latest success. That's some news! A mini-series? Who do you like for the part of Jim O'Brien? Well, yes, you really think so? Perhaps you're right. I could play myself, if you insist, if you really think I'm right for the part.

Ordinary things? You really want to hear? Well, yes, these pages are full of kidnappings and murder and death, but I would like to write of the glory of small things . . . It's just that when I do, Dr. Dalton passes me a note and sends me into a frenzy or Jammer hits me with the gas . . .

I want to be in Grenada with you.

What is true? I live in an ordinary neighborhood, I suppose, if you insist. A short walk and you are in an old town full of old houses and old porches and we all feel sleepy and old; why would I rather be out riding today?

The Frontier Remains a Dangerous Place

Tom rides. A year has passed. He knows where Alice lives and he rides the ten miles to her uncle's ranch. He had seen her in town again. She ducked her head, avoided him, afraid to be drawn back into those dread times, afraid of what he knows of her, of what her life had been with White Crane.

He is not sure of his feelings. He only knows that he can't stop thinking about her, can't speak to anyone of his feelings. He sits on his horse on the hill overlooking her cabin. Hidden in the trees, he watches in the evening as Alice and her aunt and uncle go about their chores.

He will not act upon it, but he wants to ride in, throw her up on his horse and gallop off to Mexico.

His mother and father are kind, give him chores, make him go to school, but in the evenings they turn him loose to ride his horse. At school, his main job is to watch over Will. In the beginning, he had to break up fights. Bigger, older kids would pick fights with Will, who wore buckskins. They called him

Injun Boy and other names, and soon he would be pulling Will off some screaming boy, a hunk of ear in Will's teeth.

I never start it, Will says.

But you don't have to half-kill the kids once it starts.

He fights like a wild animal. Biting, scratching, gouging for eyes. No mercy. He hurts kids years older and a hundred pounds heavier. Kids who insult him, taunt him, shove him . . .

But after a while they stop . . . Now they just avoid him . . . Give him their stony silence . . .

He's lonely. The loneliest boy on earth.

He has Tom. He's better now with his mother and father, and he likes his sister, but at night he cries himself to sleep.

Tom knows Will thinks of running off, of going back to the Comanches. Sometimes he thinks of it himself. He's lonely, too. The other kids like him, but he feels a world apart from them.

He rides his horse to the hill overlooking Alice's house. Watches over her until the light fades. Time to get back for supper. He's riding home on the wagon road when he's confronted by six young braves from the old tribe.

They surround him, three blocking the road ahead and three closing in from behind. Too late to draw his pistol. Too many of them. They know him. They're friends. Or used to be anyway.

They stand their horses in close to his. Laugh at his haircut and his clothes. They press in on him, horses snorting and tossing their heads. His hand lingers near his holster.

The braves question him about the settlement, about who lives where, the number of people in each cabin, the number of men, the kinds of weapons they have.

A lot of guns here, he says truthfully. If they hit a cabin, the Rangers would be on them before they made it back to the Red River.

They glance nervously at each other. One of them takes hold of the reins of Tom's horse. His voice turns soft and pleading: Come home with us.

Maybe I'll join up with you later.

Their faces turn sullen. Look at those clothes. Cowboy now. They hunch forward on their horses.

They ask about Will.

Dead, he says.

They were once his friends, his family. He warns them, in truth, that the Rangers are growing stronger, better armed, making more patrols.

They don't fear the army, but they fear the Rangers. They look about, eye the road north and south. He wonders if they'll kill him. Or take him. His hand drifts to the butt of his gun. They know he'll kill two or three of them anyway before they get him. They mutter, but they let him ride through.

He feels their eyes on his back. He keeps his horse walking calmly, slowly.

As he widens the distance, he kicks in his spurs at the same moment they give a war whoop. They've worked up their nerve. They're after him now.

The bullets whiz past. An arrow sticks in his saddle. Lucky they got even that close. They've mostly lost their knack with the bow and arrow. An old timer would have drilled him dead. He'd be riding right now with a two-foot shaft of arrow sticking through his breastbone. For a moment, he feels an old pride for White Crane. These young braves are just fools and incompetents compared to White Crane.

He's got a great horse, W. Ricky, tall and wide and black and fast. W. Ricky runs the race of his life, lathered and panting, Tom low over his saddle. He outdistances them, but leads them away from the cabins before turning back for home. Rides a trail to confuse them. Not that they can read tracks worth a darn, not like in the old days.

But it's only a matter of time now. They'll ride back and tell White Crane, and White Crane will come for him. White Crane will kill him and his parents and take Will back. There will be no resting now, no peace. Every moment of every day, he will be on alert. He will kill White Crane or White Crane will kill him.

The Trip to Spain

*P*icture this: a man walks through his house in the dead of night and the stupendous flatulence of his Labrador wafts over him in the hallway. The Labrador gives him a quizzical look, releases another cloud of gas. The Labrador shuts its eyes, goes back to dreaming of squirrels. The man considers writing a children's story, based on the Labrador's relationship with squirrels. There is a big brown squirrel in the backyard, king squirrel, who taunts the old dog daily, showing him its buttocks and flying up and down trees. But one day, the Labrador traps a small red squirrel, prepares to eat it. But there is something in the squirrel's eyes, something soft and innocent. He lets the squirrel run to safety. The king squirrel has witnessed this act of mercy. The king squirrel sends an emissary. Would the Labrador be willing to meet, to negotiate, to work out a treaty regarding usage of the backyard?

The man puts this story on hold, spends a restless night. His wife is snoring, her mouth exuding a not-unpleasant odor of peanut butter. His teenagers are stirring in their sleep and calling out the names of girls. Who are these girls? What dreams are his boys dreaming? What kind of father has he been? He must take the children fishing and elk hunting. He must teach them how to box.

His thoughts drift to their trip to Spain the last summer. His student Dave has suggested jazzing up the story of the trip, and the man has tried several versions, writing in the first person and in the third, but finally he decides to abandon Dave's idea, abandon making things up, and just write it as pure memoir:

> *We traveled to Spain, my wife, me, my fifteen-year-old son Leonard and my thirteen-year-old, George.*
>
> *There were some cobblestone streets going up a hill with white stucco buildings on either side of the narrow streets, and we had told the boys they could go walking on their own as long as they were back before dark, which was pretty late that time of year, oh ten P.M. or so. They had to be back at our quaint little apartment where my wife and I sat drinking sparkling water and discussing deep philosophical matters and learning interesting new things about ourselves, things we had put on hold for many years while we raised the children and focused on their needs, but we now realized it was important to work on our own relationship and I was suggesting we take off our clothes so that we might better see where we presently stood when there was a terrible rattle at the door below the apartment and we ran down to find George beating on the door and crying out that Leonard had disappeared. They had been walking when Leonard was just gone.*
>
> *He had turned his head in time to see a shape, well, it might have been more a shadow, he had a sense of more than one man somehow close, and then he looked frantically around, beat on doors, and a few people came out and scratched their*

heads and looked at him and he tried to speak Spanish and they invited him in, and he sat for a while in a kitchen with some friendly people and it occurred to him that, friendly and cheerful and helpful as they were, they knew nothing about Leonard so he ran back here to see if his older brother had returned.

But he hadn't. And my wife and I ran out with George up the hill to where Leonard had disappeared but there was no sight of him. We looked around and then went down to the police station and through some bars I saw Leonard bare from the waist up and he let out a terrible howl and I said that was my son.

The police said that he had committed a crime, but Leonard shook his head, indicating he was innocent.

I felt my wife at my side, urging me to do or say something.

Perhaps this wasn't a good idea, but I cold-cocked the policeman nearest to me, took him down with one punch and grabbed his gun and ordered the police to release Leonard at once, which they did. I took all their weapons and marched the police into the cell and locked the door. "Cool," George said. "Should we all take a gun?"

"No guns," I said. "We can't shoot our way out of this one. We're going to have to use our heads."

We recovered Leonard's shirt from a hook on the wall and we all ran out of there.

"Now what?" my wife asked.

"We'll need to change our appearances."

We stopped into a pharmacy and bought some hair dye and scissors and we went back to our apartment and changed the color of our hair and cut the kids' hair short, which I'd been wanting to do for some time anyway. By the time we got back

downtown to the bus station, though, it was obvious that we
were in trouble. There were police all over the place and they
were checking passports. There were some big dogs out. The
mood was ugly and tense and some rippling conversation went
through the crowd that there were four crazy Americans loose
somewhere in the city. We looked at each other.

We had noticed some rough streets not too far away where
drunks would simply lie down for the night and sleep it off, and
we went there, arranging ourselves as comfortably as we could
on the cobblestone streets. We passed the night uneventfully,
even got a fair night's sleep considering, and in the morning
there was a social station set up at one end of the alley and
we were given some hot coffee and donuts.

The bus station was guarded and the train station would
be as well, so we decided our best bet would be to stay in town
for a while. We went into an internet café and my children
were able to use the computer to find us a vacancy. Why yes,
it was available today.

We walked there, met a friendly man who showed us in.
But then there was something about us that alarmed him. We
didn't want to do this, but we had no choice. We tied him up
and put him in one of the beds, assuring him that we would
make sure he was safe.

My wife was starting to have some problems with all of
this. She wondered if we should consider turning ourselves in,
but the rest of us voted her down. We figured someone might
come looking for the man, so we couldn't stay here long, but
it was nice to get a breather and we all had a good shower.
We loosened the ropes on the man so that he would not be
too uncomfortable.

From there, we got on a tour bus that took us to an old cas-

tle on the edge of town. We mingled in with the other tourists and spent a pleasant day taking photos. But we noticed one of the security guards glancing our way and we became nervous.

A bunch of police with their guns drawn charged our way. We ran up some stairs and out onto a tower. We looked below, saw a glimmer of green river, and jumped. We went perfectly into the water and shot downstream. We clutched onto the side of a barge and dragged ourselves on.

The rest of it was rather simple, some time in the desert in Morocco, a period with a nomadic bandit tribe.

I guess the difficulty in telling a story like this is that people wonder if you're telling the truth or making something up. I've simply tried to tell it the way it really happened. I think we were all closer as a result. There's something about a family sticking together through a crisis.

The Therapist Weighs In

There you are on a summer's day, feeling fine, sitting in your office, when suddenly you're bent over, holding your guts, breaking into a sweat, and the next moment you're punching the walls and you know you've been had by Dr. Dalton. He's snuck something into your reading material. You're in a frenzy. As you leave the office, you hear Dalton cackling from down the hallway.

So you go to see your therapist in the room above your garage.

"You know what I fear, Jim?" the therapist says.

"What?"

"I fear you're losing your fucking mind, that's what I fear. Can I tell you a story, Jim? I grew up in Venice. Venice, California. I was just a surfer kid. Golden. Beautiful. Mindless. Getting my rocks off every night. Can you imagine the thrill of stripping a tiny bikini off a woman with an amazing body? I mean, what's better than *that*? But one day my best friend was eaten by a shark. Right in front of my eyes. One moment we were as happy as could be, riding a wave, and the next thing you know there was only a surfboard there and a pool of blood.

"My point? I see that you're expecting me to say I mended my ways, cleaned up my act. Well, I didn't. I became even more promiscuous. I became a drunk. I wandered the beach cafés and got drunk and I lowered my standards. I'd screw anyone. I screwed some real prizes. But I burned inside, Jim. I burned with pain and anger and yearning. I sought out prostitutes. I read the classics. It was meaning I wanted. Meaning. But all I found was brutal sunlight and naked flesh. Am I boring you, Jim? Actually our time is up. Leave a check on the desk and close the door quietly."

"But I live here."

"Who asked for your opinion?"

The Story of the Major

Time to go boxing.

He's talking about the real boxing. He's not talking about a couple of lean, well-trained guys fighting for millions of bucks.

He's talking about a couple of middle-aged guys flailing away at each other in a palooka gym until Jim falls to one knee, gasping, not because he's been hit but because he's out of breath, and there's no one to cheer, no one to yell: Get up, you lunk!

So he has to hear that voice inside. And just why the hell should he get up anyway? There he is, caught in an existential dilemma. Get up, why? No money at stake. Past pride. Past hope. Listening to his own breath whistle raggedly. Wheezing. Heart pounds. This could all be over. He could easily say, "That's enough today." Get up, why?

Perhaps images of his entire life sweep over him as he pauses there on a knee, considering . . . Oh, probably not. Just how quickly does the subconscious work after all, and isn't that a big load really, a big fictional load that allows characters to have these enormous breathtaking revelations and lyrical flashbacks and flashforwards all in a matter of seconds and what probably goes through Jim's mind as he rests on one knee, panting, is the simple thought: I'm going to have a heart attack . . . The gym coach asks, "Are you going to get up, Jim? Do you want to call it a day?"

Why the hell should he get up? But for the hell of it, let's say that he is swept by images of his life. Let's go ahead and say that he is remembering a sports glory day of his youth. He's seventeen and a senior, graduating in a month. He didn't play on the football team the last couple of years, had a run-in with his coach. But he's in a pick-up game with some of the guys from the team. They're toast. They can't tackle him. They lunge futilely at him. His short powerful legs propel him through their grasping arms, and they know he's the best player out there even if he didn't play on the team. He had the best trainer there ever was, his brother Len. Len showed him everything there was to know about football, played with him so many afternoons and evenings he'd grown fast and cagey chasing Len, dodging Len. This is it. This is all the sports glory he'll ever have—this day. He won't make an eighty-yard run in the Rose Bowl. He will not be featured in *Sports Illustrated*. And even Cicely will not be there to throw herself into his arms and whisper: *My hero*. But on an evening in April, as his senior year draws to a close, he will have this. This moment.

They play late into the evening. It's too late in the year to worry about studying. They'll all graduate anyway. The war's winding down, the draft over. No worries for the future. So they've got this, this long afternoon and evening and into the gloom of dusk as they play and play and play, the real football, the unpadded tackle football. As the other boys, the players from the team, grow weak and tired, he grows stronger with each run, surges with power and energy, makes cuts that he's never made before, cuts that no one has ever made—leaves one hip behind, separates his thighs from his knees. And finally makes no cuts at all, just plows over them, drags eight or nine players across the field. He's unstoppable. His own teammates join the other side. He plays alone against twenty of them. Still, they can't stop him. They mutter among themselves. Their own accomplishments seem as straw. And yet, they are exhilarated, too. They have touched greatness this day, this spring evening as the light fades.

And Jim O'Brien, on one knee on the canvas in a palooka gym in a small city somewhere in the West, is swept by images of that day. So is it some dream of glory that makes him rise from the canvas?

No, no dream of glory. But maybe he wishes to honor that young man of many years before, and so he rises.

"Are you sure?" Ron, the gym coach, asks. "Do you still have the gas?"

"I've got plenty of gas," he says, and he lets out one to show them.

"Geez," Ron says, waving his hand to ward off the malodorous fumes which waft over the ring.

"Hey, let's stop," his boxing partner Pete says, "if you're going to fight that way."

Voice thick through the mouth guard, Jim says, "Let's go."

And they go on, beating the living daylights out of each other. Later, Pete will go back to his job as a certified public accountant, but for now these two middle aged men are boxing, the real and the true boxing in a dead end gym in a forgotten corner of the world.

Brief interview on *60 Minutes* with football players from the day in question:

Frank R.: "I wouldn't describe it quite like that."

John S: "I remember something. I mean the guy could play. When he wanted to. He was kind of a loafer as I recall."

Ronnie C: "It's bull. If he was that good, why didn't he play on the team?"

Arnold W: "Yeah, it was pretty much what happened. It was one of the most amazing things I've ever witnessed. Not that big a guy, and he dragged us all across the field. He whipped our asses."

Bobby G (laughing): "We went to school together? To tell the truth, I don't remember him at all."

Back in the boxing gym, Pete, who may be a ringer, ex-Golden Gloves or something, hammers him in the forehead, and Jim sinks to a knee again.

Pete stands over him, bounces on his toes, blue mouthguard full of foam, blood at the rims of his nose. "I'm sorry, Jim. Are you okay?"

Which is good boxing. Which is good attitude boxing. None of this prancing around stuff, taunting your opponent, snapping your teeth and beating your chest.

Good manners is what real boxing is all about.

He pants. Down on one knee, forearm across thigh. And as he pauses there, more images and flashbacks sweep over him.

He's at a sleepover at his friend's house, a Vietnamese kid adopted by an American fighter pilot, a Major. He's a tiny, slender kid, but he grew up fighting to survive in the orphanage, and when a bully at the parochial school pesters him, he drops to a squatting position and grabs hold of his testicles, latches on with both hands and squeezes with steely little fingers. Ignores punches and kicks and squeezes until the bully collapses and blubbers for mercy, beating in agony at the warm grass of the playground, the steely fingers still squeezing. Squeezing. Squeezing, while the bully sobs and writhes in the grass, kicking his feet and blubbering. No one bullies him after that.

Jim's asleep with his friend on sleeping bags on the living room floor. He wakes in the night to find the Major lying beside him, sprawled over him, heavy leg draped over him, pinning him. The Major touches him, strokes and fondles his penis.

Jim freezes. The Major's been like a best old friend to him, an uncle, a second father. Fighter pilot. Rugged. Handsome. Sometimes he gives the boys a beer. That's better for you than Coke, he says.

Maybe it's the memory of doing nothing, of saying nothing, of lying there and letting the Major stroke his penis in a cool, detached sort of way, as if stroking the penis of your son's best friend is a perfectly normal, perfectly natural thing to do. Maybe it's the memory of that and the subsequent times before he learned to avoid the Major, see him coming and think, whoops, let's get away from Mr. Hand, Mr. Hand in the Night Man, Mr. Hand in the Kitchen Man, Mr. Hand Whenever You Can Man, so long Mr. Hand, before he learned to escape, to fade away, he let the hand touch him through the course of a long year when a kid ought to be just hitting his stride, coming into the world cool and solid and full of juice and pride instead of having Mr. Hand Man take the pride and the cool and confidence out of him all with the stroke of a hand.

It's that memory that makes him rise up once again from the canvas and say, "Let's go. Let's box."

"Come on now," Pete says. "You're hurt."

"I'm going to call it," Ron says.

But he flurries back in before Ron can end it.

He's got the gas back, the juice, the stuff.

"Well okay, then," Pete says, backpedaling. They go around the ring in good time.

"Well, okay," Ron says. "Looking good. Looking good for a couple of old guys."

And that's boxing, boys. That's the real and the true boxing.

And now Jim flashes back on a night in the suburbs. Our seventeen-year-old hero, Jim, is at a party. He's a surfer. Not that he has ever surfed. But if your hair is long, flips up in the back, curls over your ears, but it's not long enough to qualify you as a hippie, you're a surfer. It's a party of surfers. A kegger. Some kid's parents out for the night. The party has spilled out of the backyard and into the front yard. A couple of pickup trucks full of cowboys pull up to the curb of the house. Not that they're real cowboys. But they've got the boots and the hats anyway. They pile out of the trucks, and the surfers, chickenshits that they are, scream and holler and run inside—all except for Jim. He thinks of what Len would do. He makes a lone stand. He stands on the front lawn, holding his spot of lawn. His turf. A while ago, he had puked almost right on this spot. He has claimed this land, not through his blood, but through his puke.

They surround him. Fifteen or so. No problem. He's seen the movie *Billy Jack*. "I'll fight one of you," he offers.

"Nah," one of the cowboys says. "It will be a lot easier if we all just jump you."

Well, not such a great spot on the lawn anyway. If you get right down to it, not much of a lawn. Hell, this ain't the Alamo.

He breaks through their skirmish line—a halfback on the run of his life. Around the house, into the darkness, pursued, smacks into a swing set, wipes out a wooden kid's fort, and that's football, folks, that's the real and the true football. Trapped now by a chain link fence, starts scrambling over it. They drag him down. A royal beating. Flurry of fists. Down on the ground and boots thud into his ribs. No real pain yet. But serious stuff. He lets out an enormous fake cry of agony, really belts it out, makes a death rattle sound in his throat.

"We killed him!" one cries. They run off in panic.

He rises to a knee, bloody, shirt torn, stumbling into the future. Showed *them*! Now that's fighting, boys, that's fighting.

"Hey," Pete protests. "Easy," he mumbles through his mouthguard. "Are you trying to kill me?"

"Easy," Ron says, "Easy. I got liability issues."

Driving home from the boxing ring, many years too late, he says to the Major, "It wasn't that you touched me. It was that you betrayed me. You were my friend. You were like a second father to me."

The Major shrugs. "I touched a lot of boys. What makes you so special?"

The Major fades away, and old Ernie drives around with Jim in his car. It is suddenly winter. That's the way it is with Ernie sometimes. They drive through the snowy streets. He's wearing a fishing hat. He's handsome, a moustache, but no famous white beard, the pre-Papa days. That famous wide jaw. What a jaw, that jaw could take a punch.

"So did you know you'd be great?" Jim asks. "Did you always know? When did you know?"

"Oh, I guess I always knew," he says. Jim hears a rumble in his voice. It's a good voice, a good and a true voice.

"When I was a kid," Ernie says, "I felt . . . "

"Destined?"

"That's a big word," he says, "Destined. It's a good word, but it picks you up and drops you just as far. Destined. That's a big word."

"So you always knew?"

"A lot of guys know."

"But it doesn't work out for most of them."

"Things go wrong. You catch a bullet. A leftie drops you. A bull hooks you."

"What was it with you and Fitz anyway?"

"Ah." He sounds sad now. "I loved Scottie. He always misunderstood me. That's a big word, misunderstood. But it's a good enough and a true enough word. He thought I wanted him to be tougher, more manly. That's a big word, manly, not in the number of letters, which are few, five in total, but in meaning. He caught himself performing for me, and he hated himself for it. All I wanted was for him to be himself. To be the real Scottie. The real and the true Scottie."

"That thing with the penis?"

"That never happened. Not like that. He wanted to be tough for me. He wanted to box."

"To box you?"

"He didn't show me his penis. He showed me his fist. He wanted to know if his fist was too small."

"Was it?"

He shrugs. "I've seen lightweights do okay with small fists. What are you, one-sixty?"

"About."

"You could drop to one-forty-seven. You'd do better in a lower division."

"You think so?"

He reaches across Jim's chest. Unbuckles his seat belt, opens his door and shoves him out of the moving car. He drops into a snowbank. Ernie slides behind the wheel and takes off driving Jim's car, fishing hat low over his brow.

Later he joins Jim at a sidewalk café in Paris. The car's lost, Jim supposes.

Ernie drinks a Pernod. "This brings you up," he says. "But it drops you just as far. What are you drinking?"

"Coffee."

"That stuff will kill you. Won't you have one with me, Scottie?"

"I gave it all up."

"Just one, little dick?"

Ernie gets blasted, incoherent. Slugs a waiter. One of his wives drags him off and Jim's back here in a supermarket, looking at a cover of a magazine that holds out, in this tormented world, the possibility of acquiring a knockout butt. The kind of hard, high-riding butt that one can be proud of.

And now he remembers Ernie's last words before he slipped into incoherence. "I was always misunderstood," he said. "The war stuff, the hunting, the fishing, the boxing, the bullfighting. All the tough guy stuff. All I really wanted was one thing. To make beauty. To make beauty out of the ordinary little things."

For Your Eyes Only

J have decided to write more of ordinary things. I won't write about kidnappings and murders for a while. I have decided to write about small things. I have decided to share my journal of our RV trip a couple of summers ago. It was an ordinary trip. If it had not been ordinary, I would not tell you about it. This is a man who lives in a most ordinary way! So ordinary that he is astonishing!

JUNE 29

Mileage in rented RV stands at 1,041. We set forth at 12:40 P.M. Good luck and godspeed.

Topped off in Fort Garland. $28.00. From time to time there is a disturbing rattle in the RV.

We arrived at Great Sand Dunes. Had a good time walking and running through dunes, which stretch on for miles and miles. Reminded us of the movie *Lawrence of Arabia*. It is very tiring to run up a sand dune. Boys tried to slide on cardboard boxes, but met with limited success. Would slide about for a foot and then pitch off into the sand. We gave this up after a little while.

In the evening, I was bit on the arm by a rattlesnake. I opened the wound with a knife, sucked up the venom, spat it out. Ellen poured a little rubbing alcohol on the wound. The boys brought some ice from the cooler. It swelled up a little and I took a couple of ibuprofen.

We stayed the night at San Luis State Park (SITE 13). SITE 13 was beautiful, on the outside of the loop. Nice place. There was a basketball court with a very short basket. We enjoyed dunking the ball on the short basket. We are a short family. We'd never been able to dunk before. Boys and I had a good time playing. Ellen made spectacular dinner in RV kitchen—spicy chicken with rice. We watched the first half of an old movie with Henry Fonda, *Drums Along the Mohawk*. Just outside the RV, a mountain lion was trying to devour a deer. The boys peppered it with BBs, and the lion ran away. The deer came up to the door and we petted it and bandaged its leg and gave it some Cheerios.

JUNE 30

Spent night at Mesa Verde. First backing up in RV we took out a mesquite tree and a cooking grill. Saw big wild turkey. Had fun playing football with boys. Ellen made great dinner of hamburger, rice, and salad. Finished *Drums Along the Mohawk*. Long poetic scene of Henry Fonda being chased by three fast Indians with tomahawks.

JULY 1

Crossing Painted Desert, rusted red earth. Series of mesas, phallic shaped buttes, gullies and washes; see smoke on north rim of Grand Canyon.

2,106 miles. Needles, Arizona. $58.00 gas.

Spent night at Grand Canyon National Park. A trailer village.

Not much privacy, but a good spot near canyon rim. We walked along the rim. We were all impressed by the grandeur.

Boys bickered a lot all afternoon, but finally settled down. I spoke to them about their bickering and they informed me that they do not bicker as much as some of their friends. For instance, Alex keeps a loaded BB gun next to his bed and shoots at his brother Ben if he comes into the room.

July 2

Today a hot drive across Mojave Desert. Boys in good spirits, though listless. Lounge on RV couches as I drive. Reminds me of long ago family trip. Wave of nostalgia sweeps over me. I look at the two boys, the brothers. I pray they will always stay well, stay friends, stay close.

$38.00 2,282 miles. A little past Barstow.

Mcgave. $48.00. 2,338 miles.

Somewhere $31.00 2,479 miles.

Spent a lovely night at San Felipe State Park. A little south of San Jose. Beautiful lake and hills. Built campfire and cooked marshmallows. Saw some fireworks from small town in distance. Suggested singing old Beatles songs. *In the town where I was born, lived a man who sailed to sea . . .* We notice a bear watching from nearby. He seems like a well-meaning bear with a good attitude.

July 3

Spent nice day in San Francisco at Fisherman's Wharf. Rode cable cars and walked up and down steep streets. Boys went to Ripley's Believe it or Not museum. Talked afterwards about a man who could pull strings through his nose.

Some rough driving through Golden Gate Park and up Highway 101. We gave up on the hairpin turns on Highway 101, turned back and drove for hours until late at night we found a motel on Highway 5. Had a big room, and boys went swimming in pool in morning. A heavy man fainted and fell in and went to the bottom and the boys dragged him out and successfully administered CPR from having seen it on a TV show. In the fall we were invited back to town for an award ceremony where we met the Mayor, a jolly fellow.

July 4–10

We go up to Oregon and hang out at the cabin in the little country town with Grandma and Grandpa. We show off our RV. The boys' cousins next door sneak in and pee in our RV toilet. We play badminton in the evenings.

I like the way the boys set up their area in the loft and the way they look lying in their beds which are arranged side by side. They ride bikes to the store each day to rent a movie. It makes me happy when they're upstairs at night in the loft watching a movie after the rest of us have turned in. I like sneaking up the stairs and watching them for a little while. They usually notice me and say, "Hi, Dad" and I think they're happy that I stay and watch them for a couple of minutes, but I also think they're happy when I don't stay too long.

We went to a quilt show on the Fourth of July weekend. Ellen bought a pretty quilt, though not the golfer's quilt. Still, I look forward to pulling the quilt over me in the coming winter.

We stay in the cabin, but sometimes I sneak back into the RV to take a piss.

July 11

Heading home. George begins to sing old Beatles songs. His high voice is a delight. Must record before it changes. (I fail to do this and his voice changes and I must try to recall that delightful high singing voice.)

At a road rest area, he gets his hands in sap somehow; the sap gets onto his shirt. He protests, "I hate being sticky!" I remark to Ellen that I had not known before that he hated being sticky. She reminded me that he washes his hands at restaurants when they get sticky. Then he announces, "Now my nose is bleeding!" It has been a rough stop.

July 12

Stopped in Boise for gas. $50.00.

July 13

$48.00 gas. 3,875 mileage.

640 mile drive yesterday. Spent last night in weedy camp. Happy to move on.

July 13

$48.00 gas in Rock Springs.

July 14

Home again, home again.

July 16

Go in for physical. Doctor recommends that the next time I am bit by a rattlesnake, I promptly seek medical attention.

The Long Way Home

When Jim opens his office door and turns on the light, he is startled to see Dr. Dalton already sitting there. He has been lurking in the darkness, waiting for him.

He holds up a flashcard with letters on it. Jim looks at it without reacting. He checks himself for signs of agitation. He looks in triumphant serenity at Dalton. "It doesn't work on me anymore," he says. "You see, I have read something of yours and had no reaction."

Dalton gives him a toothy grin. "I was hoping you'd say that. That was the control card! Now try this!" He holds up a second card and Jim staggers back. He is filled with rage. Dr. Dalton has already disappeared, cackling down the hallway.

Jim's going to see President Jammer. He's going to tell him off. He's sick of this place. He's sick of the mediocrity they have all slipped into, slip into more deeply with each passing day. He wants something, something he can't name.

Resolve and rage sends him forth and crossing the quadrangle, he smells the acrid whiff of gas and as he gets closer to Jammer's building, the white gas comes leaking out of the bushes and he knows he will not be stopped, and even when he falls, he knows when he rises he will stagger on to Jammer's office and give him the fisherman's toss out the window.

But for now Jim floats through the sky and is carried back to the frontier, carried back to see Tom on his horse above the hill over Alice's house. It is night, and as he watches the house, he detects motion, and realizes there is a hit going down on the cabin—seven Comanches sneaking in and now whooping and beating on the doors and windows. He doesn't think White Crane is along. White Crane has stopped raiding the settlements. Besides, White Crane would lead a classier attack. He doubts that White Crane knows Alice is inside or he would have found a more clever way of capturing her.

He draws his gun and charges in on W. Ricky, but the Comanches have already beaten down the door and they throw Alice up on a horse. Tom drops three of them as they ride off.

That leaves four and he rides after them, reloading his gun as he rides. Dropping more of them, coming closer, W. Ricky panting and slathering and slobbering and Tom firing and it comes to him as he charges through the night that he has become the Hound of Death.

He shoots down the last Indian, and he pulls Alice from her horse and embraces her.

They are married in a quiet wedding in the settlements, and move into their own cabin not far from Edmund and Rebecca's cabin.

But Will . . . Though Tom spends time with him, it is not the same. Will is the loneliest boy on earth. One night he slips out, mounts his horse and rides back to White Crane's village.

White Crane is ecstatic. They have many feasts. But White Crane begins to brood. Tom and Alice are traitors. What of

Will? Will he turn back one day, desert White Crane again? Is he really a Comanche?

He gives Will a test. They must ride back to the settlements and kill Tom and Alice.

With sorrow and anguish, Will rides along. At night they are above Tom and Alice's cabin. White Crane tells Will to hold the horses. On foot White Crane goes stealthily down with five braves.

Will draws his gun. When White Crane and the other braves have disappeared into the darkness, he pulls the trigger and fires three shots into the air, signaling the alarm to the cabin below.

White Crane comes running back with the braves. He pants, breathless, as the other braves move in around Will with their knives drawn. He had needed to know this. He draws his own knife, and as the other braves close in on Will, White Crane moves in front of Will, blocking them, holding them off.

The braves seethe, but they wait for White Crane to make his move. White Crane holds his shoulders. The boy trembles, waiting for the knife. White Crane makes a strange, strangled sound in his throat.

He presses his lips to Will's forehead. Touches with his hand to rub the kiss deep inside.

White Crane mounts his horse. He does not look back. He gives a command and the braves follow him, their shoulders slumped, for the last time riding slowly away from the settlements.

Will rides his horse downhill. Years have passed from when he was first taken. Tom opens the door and he and Will stand there looking at one another. Tom takes Will into his arms and they stand in the doorway, hugging one another as Alice stands behind, not quite knowing what to do, crying, touching at their heads, their shoulders.

Will and Tom live to be old men. At parties for children and grandchildren and great grandchildren, Will arrives in buckskin outfits, and at the age of eighty he amuses the kids by walking across the lawn on his hands.

Some recall a laughing, funny man, but some say that he always seemed lonely, as if there were no place on this earth that he really belonged.

THE END OF THE
O'BRIEN FAMILY SAGA

A Night at the Y

Stories by Robert Garner McBrearty

978-1-942280-02-6
$12.99

Wild, funny, touching, and full of crackling dialogue, Robert Garner McBrearty's stories turn the intensity of life up a notch, creating a heightened reality that is both hilarious and heartbreakingly real. His characters struggle to hold onto work, love, and sanity, and wrestle with the choice of whether to be responsible citizens and family men or heroic hellraisers who run with the bulls.

MORE GREAT BOOKS FROM CONUNDRUM PRESS

Let the Birds Drink in Peace

Stories by Robert Garner McBrearty

978-0-9713678-2-1
$14.99

"What threads through McBrearty's work is a humaneness toward his characters and a gentle, sometimes sad irony . . . He is as adept at moving the reader with an understanding of life's more poignant moments as he is at making one laugh."

—Robin Hemley, *Chicago Tribune*